PULCINELLA

Indiana Pulcinella

OTHER DETECTIVE LANE MYSTERIES
Queen's Park
The Lucky Elephant Restaurant
A Hummingbird Dance
Smoked
Malabarista
Foxed
Glycerine

OTHER NEWEST MYSTERIES
Business As Usual, by Michael Boughn
The Cardinal Divide, by Stephen Legault
The Darkening Archipelago, by Stephen Legault
A Deadly Little List, by K. Stewart & C. Bullock
A Magpie's Smile, by Eugene Meese
Murder in the Chilcotin, by Roy Innes
Murder in the Monashees, by Roy Innes
West End Murders, by Roy Innes

FOR MORE ON THESE AND OTHER TITLES,
VISIT NEWESTPRESS.COM

Garry Ryan

INDIANA
PULCINELLA

A Detective Lane Mystery

**A NeWest
Mystery**

COPYRIGHT © GARRY RYAN 2016

LIBRARY AND ARCHIVES CANADA CATALOGUING IN PUBLICATION

Ryan, Garry, 1953–, author
Indiana pulcinella / Garry Ryan.

Issued in print and electronic formats.
ISBN 978-1-926455-57-0 (paperback). — ISBN 978-1-926455-58-7 (epub). —
ISBN 978-1-926455-59-4 (mobi)

I. Title.

PS8635.Y354I54 2016   C813'.6   C2015-906552-6
                                              C2015-906553-4

Editor for the Board: Leslie Vermeer
Cover and interior design: Natalie Olsen, Kisscut Design
Cover photo: Natalie Olsen, Kisscut Design
Author photo: Luke Towers

NeWest Press acknowledges the support of the Canada Council for the Arts, the Alberta Foundation for the Arts, and the Edmonton Arts Council for support of our publishing program. We acknowledge the financial support of the Government of Canada through the Canada Book Fund for our publishing activities.

#201, 8540–109 Street
Edmonton, Alberta T6G 1E6
780.432.9427
NeWest Press www.newestpress.com

No bison were harmed in the making of this book.
Printed and bound in Canada

for
KARMA,
BEN,
and
LUKE

"That is the life."

— Mafalda Stamile

chapter 1

"What are you doing here?" Lori leaned on the doorframe marking the entrance and exit to Lane and Nigel's office. Lori wore a pair of red knee-high boots, a black skirt, a blue satin blouse, and an attitude. She ran the office, keeping detectives in line and taking a few under her wing.

Lane — remarkable because the six-foot-tall detective appeared so unremarkable — looked at Nigel Li, who sat at the next desk. Nigel raised his black eyebrows, locking his hands behind his neck then rubbing the back of his close-shaved head.

I'm on my own, Lane thought.

Lori shook her head, sighing. "Your nephew Matt called. Your presence is required at the hospital."

Lane stood up, reaching for the inside pocket of his grey sports jacket. He pulled out his phone. Its face told him he'd missed multiple calls. He looked at Lori, holding up the phone. "But it didn't ring."

Nigel rolled his office chair next to Lane and took the phone, flicking a switch on the side. "Ringer's off." He handed the phone back to his greying partner and looked at Lori. "He just got it yesterday." Nigel tapped Lane on the arm of his mauve shirt. "You've also got a text message."

Lane took a second look at the face of his phone, seeing the message from Matt. The text message window asked, "Where the hell are you?"

"Foothills Medical Centre. Fifth floor. They'll direct you from there." Lori turned sideways in the doorway. "Repeat it."

Lane put on his sports jacket, then his winter coat. "Foothills, fifth floor."

Nigel stood, adjusting the back of Lane's collar as he made for the door. They were about the same height with a twenty-year age difference.

Lori put her heels against one side of the doorframe. Lane turned sideways to go through the doorway. For an instant they stood eye to eye.

Lori smiled. "Don't worry. You're not my type."

Lane began to laugh. When he got into the Chev parked at the fenced-in police lot, he was still smiling. *Why am I so wired?* He manoeuvred his way out of downtown by driving under the Centre Street Bridge and over the Bow River. He turned west onto Memorial Drive, thinking about how he'd come to this point. He and his partner Arthur had inherited nephew Matt and then Christine, a niece. Both were teens discarded by their families. Now Christine and boyfriend Daniel were having a baby, and life was about to become even more complicated.

Fifteen minutes later he was parked out front of the Foothills Medical Centre. Within the cluster of buildings stood the original hospital, its three wings roughly in the shape of a Y. Lane locked the car and headed for the entrance, careful not to slip on patches of ice or get run over by people searching for parking spots while talking on their phones. He passed a man wearing a housecoat sitting in a wheelchair. An oxygen tank hung off the rear of the chair. The man lifted a lighter from his lap, lighting what appeared to be a cigarette. He closed his eyes as he inhaled, exhaling smoke and vapour to cloud the mountain air.

Lane recognized the pungent aroma of marijuana. The man pressed the joint between his index and middle fingers, giving Lane a wave with his free hand.

Lane nodded, crossed the street in front of the hospital, and stepped inside. He stamped the snow off his feet under a blast of hot air between the two sets of automatic sliding glass doors. Inside, people lined up for coffee to his right, walked the corridor to Emergency, walked the hallway to the Tom Baker Cancer Centre, bought cards and gifts at a tiny shop, stood waiting in front of the elevators.

Lane stood behind a pregnant woman whose male attendant carried an overnight bag. The woman was taller than Lane and wore a pink T-shirt with a white arrow pointing to BABY. The fabric on the T-shirt was stretched so the arrow was distorted at its point. The woman bent forward, putting her hands on her knees and moaning while her companion rubbed her back. Lane tried not to notice the crack in her backside when the top of her sweatpants drooped.

He followed them into the elevator.

"Fifth floor! Robbie! Fifth floor!" the woman said. Robbie pressed the button. "OOOOOOH!" she said as the doors closed and the elevator climbed. "Ooooooh." The elevator bounced to a stop, and the doors opened.

Lane followed Robbie, who followed his mate.

The men were content to trail in her wake until Robbie slipped and recovered, Lane veered to one side, and the woman stopped. "My water broke!"

A pair of metal doors stood in her way. On the right was an admittance window.

"Comin' through!" The woman punched the big round metal button and the doors opened.

"Wait!" The woman behind the counter grabbed the phone and said, "She just went right through!"

Lane followed the pair to the nurses' desk.

The woman said, "We need a room!"

A tiny grey-haired nurse stood up from behind the counter, looked at the pregnant woman, saw the wet crotch of her sweatpants, and smiled. "A little late for that, wouldn't you say?" The nurse focused on Robbie and pointed left. "Five zero two. A nurse will be there right away."

Lane looked up at the names on the white board, spotted Christine's, then headed for her room.

He found his partner Arthur in the hallway. Arthur was looking thinner around the middle and his scalp shone on top. His brown eyes stared at a closed door. He turned as Lane approached. Arthur's face was drawn, and there were dark patches under his eyes.

"You're here." Arthur held out his hand. Lane took it.

A nurse rolled a cart down the hall, parking it in front of the door to Christine's room. Lane and Arthur stared at a pair of paddle-shaped metal instruments.

"What are those?" Lane asked.

"Forceps, I think." Arthur released Lane's hand.

Lane nodded, tried looking away from the forceps, found he could not. His index and forefinger worried away at what was left of an earlobe. "Where are Matt and Dan?"

"Dan's in the room. Matt's gone to get some coffee." Arthur resumed staring at the door.

"So you walk right by and pretend like you don't know me." Matt walked or rather shuffled/skipped/hopped down the hallway; his CP gait was so unique it was often hard to tell what exactly he was doing. Still wearing his winter jacket, he held out a tray of coffees. When everyone had taken a cup, Matt turned to dump the tray in the garbage.

Lane asked, "What about a coffee for Dan?"

"I'm not going in there!" Strawberry-blond, brown-eyed Matt stood about the same height as Lane and about three inches taller than Arthur, but he was obviously intimidated by whatever was happening behind the closed door.

Arthur said, "Thanks for the coffee."

"Yes, thank you." Lane took a sip.

The three of them stood watching the door while nurses walked in and out of Christine's room. A doctor arrived. She looked to be about thirty-five and weighed about one hundred thirty pounds, with red hair and a face that would launch more than a thousand ships.

Fifteen minutes later, Dan opened the door, smiling. "He's here." Then he stepped back into the room.

A nurse pushed a cart topped with a clear plastic crib out of the room. A head full of black hair was visible at the top of a blanket.

Lane looked at the pale face of a boy, frowning at the lights.

The nurse said, "Don't worry, we'll get him cleaned up. He's going to NICU. You'll be able to visit him soon." She wheeled the cart down the hall.

Lane's phone beeped.

Matt asked, "Uncle? You okay?"

Lane wiped the tears from his cheeks, nodding. His phone beeped again. He pulled it from his pocket.

Arthur shook his head, reading the number on Lane's phone. "*Kharra alhikum.* They can give us a fucking hour, can't they?"

Matt grinned at Arthur. "Way to tell 'em, Uncle!"

The text message was from Chief Jim Simpson. "See me ASAP."

Dan opened the door again and stepped out. He was taller than the three other men and had brown hair. His eyes were underlined with fatigue.

"How is she?" Lane asked.

"Tired and happy." Dan let his chin drop.

"Congratulations, Dad!" Matt said.

Dan raised his head and smiled. "He's beautiful."

Lane's phone rang. He looked at the number, then looked at Arthur, who shook his head then sighed. "It's Lori." Lane answered. "Hello."

"Well? Is the baby born yet? You said you'd call as soon as you knew," Lori said.

"Yes. The little guy was just born." Lane smiled at Dan.

"Good. Congratulations. I was asked to get hold of you. We need you," Lori said.

×

Chief Jim Simpson's administrative secretary Jean had immaculate short grey hair. She waved at Lane while pointing at the Chief's door.

Lane nodded, opened the door, stepped inside, and closed it.

Simpson frowned from where he sat across the coffee table. His close-cut blond hair and thin face gave him a boyish quality, despite some grey, but his eyes were a different matter. There was determination there, and an underlying anger.

Nigel Li sat across from the Chief. His head shone beneath the five o'clock shadow of thick black hair. He was tall and barbed-wire thin with a long-standing reputation for his prickly tongue. "There you are."

Is that relief I hear in your voice? Lane wondered.

There was a knock at the door. Lane turned, Jean handed him a cup of coffee, he took it, and the door shut once more.

"Sit down, please," Simpson said.

Lane sat down between the pair, putting his coffee on the table.

Nigel said, "We've got a —"

Simpson threw his hand up, snapping the palm open in Nigel's face. Nigel's eyes narrowed.

Lane looked at Nigel, nodding. *Just listen. This isn't the time to piss off the Chief.*

Nigel sat back.

Simpson said, "We have a double murder, husband and wife, last name Randall. He's the CEO of an energy company, and she's a benefactor of the arts. The pair were executed, the house was robbed, and their dog was nailed to the wall." He waited.

Lane looked out the window and across to the curved glass of the city's tallest building. The words of an old friend, Deputy Chief Cam Harper, came back to him: "We keep turning over rocks and finding another pile of shit left by Smoke." Then Lane remembered former Chief Smoke facing the cameras when he said, "The speedy arrest of the suspect in these murders means Calgarians can sleep easier tonight."

Simpson watched Lane make the connection to similar murders, then nodded.

Nigel opened his mouth.

Simpson held up his hand again.

Lane turned to Nigel. "Three years ago, a well-connected couple was killed, their dog hung on the wall, and the house robbed. A schizophrenic homeless man named Byron Thomas confessed to the crime. It was a feather in Smoke's cap. His guys made the arrest and got a confession. Thomas ended up in jail."

It was Nigel's turn to look out the window at the city's tallest building.

Simpson said, "I need you on this case but can't tell you to take it. Whichever way it goes, it'll cost you. Smoke's old-boy network is still entrenched, and this case has the potential to embarrass them. If you take it, there will likely be a price to pay somewhere down the road."

Nigel said, "Not everyone looks at it that way."

Lane sat back and thought, *Okay, Nigel. Go with it. I just hope this doesn't blow up in your face.*

Simpson's face flushed. He turned his eyes on the young officer, taking a deep breath. "What does that mean?"

Nigel looked Lane in the eye and said, "Most of the younger members of the CPS have a different take on this."

Simpson reached for his coffee, taking a sip.

Nigel continued. "Most of them have worked with Smoke's good ol' boys. A few liked being part of the network, but most welcomed the change after Smoke resigned. And you might be surprised at how many of the older officers like the way Lane stood up to Smoke." He looked out the window as if waiting to be contradicted.

Simpson put his coffee down, taking another long breath. "Will the pair of you take this one on?" He looked at Lane and waited.

Lane looked at Nigel, who nodded. Lane said, "Okay."

Simpson put his coffee on the table, looking at Lane. "I hear congratulations are in order. Your niece had a boy?"

Lane smiled. "Just saw him this morning."

Simpson asked, "Mom and baby okay?"

"He's in NICU. Something called meconium aspiration syndrome. They have him on antibiotics. The nurses say he'll be fine."

Chief Simpson frowned. "Does this make you a great-uncle?"

Lane shrugged. "Just happy."

Simpson looked at Nigel. "You two can say no."

Nigel looked at Lane, who said, "It's our job."

The Chief handed Lane an address. Lane glanced at the paper and said, "It's about two blocks from where I grew up."

×

Nigel drove the unmarked grey Chev up the hill, guiding them away from the river valley along Crowchild Trail. The pavement was cleared of snow but not of black ice. He asked, "Is your house big enough for a baby?"

Lane watched a panel van slip and grip in the right lane. "Christine, Daniel, and the baby will have the bottom level, we all share the kitchen, and Matt moved upstairs. I imagine it will be kind of crazy until we all adjust."

"How do Dan's parents fit into the picture?"

"That's a good question. Christine and Dan's mother have this tempestuous relationship."

Nigel eased into the right lane. "Tempestuous?"

How come so many questions? "Lola's a successful business woman who likes control. Christine doesn't like to be controlled."

"Oh." Nigel nodded, easing onto a ramp, then a side street.

Seven minutes later, they arrived in front of a stylish yet understated two-storey home renovated to accommodate the established neighbourhood's architecture. Nigel parked behind the Forensic Crime Scene Unit. They looked at the house and its coat of snow. A freshly shovelled twenty-foot front driveway led to a two-car garage set beneath the right side of the house. Lane saw it was the smallest in a neighbourhood of three- and four-car garages.

Lane stepped out of the Chev, looking around. The limbs of mature evergreens sagged under the weight of snow. Here and there, smoke plumes rose from chimneys. Beneath the chimneys stood four- and five-thousand-square-foot homes, custom-built or extensively renovated. Some were stuccoed, some had brick faces, and one was made of sandstone. A few driveways and curbs were dotted with older Mercedes and BMWs. *Not many domestic cars in sight in this part of the city.*

A garage door opened, a starter whined, and an engine coughed and caught. Lane watched a silver Mercedes SUV backing out of a garage. Its tires crunched over the snow. The woman behind the wheel looked to be thirty-something. She spotted Lane and looked away.

He walked toward the vehicle when she stopped in the street, shifting into drive. She was facing him. He could see that she was blonde, her eyes were blue, and her left hand gripped the top of the steering wheel. A substantial engagement ring glittered next to a diamond-encrusted wedding band flashing in the sunlight. Lane glanced to his right. The sun sat just above the rooftop of the victims' home.

Lane reached into his pocket and pulled out his ID, holding it up.

The woman slouched into her seat, her shoulders fell, and she mouthed a curse.

Lane walked up to the driver's door of the silver Mercedes. He stood on the other side of the glass, waiting a full thirty seconds before an electric motor whirred and the window rolled halfway down. The subtle scent of perfume mixed with leather. Lane saw skin tightly stretched over cheekbones and sunken eyes. *I was off by thirty years. She's at least sixty-five.*

"I'm late for a hair appointment," the woman said.

"How well do you know the Randalls?" Lane asked.

"I did know them." The woman nodded in the direction of the house.

Word games. I'm tired of this already. "Name?" He waited before he said, "Please."

"Do I need a lawyer?" The woman sat up straighter, attempting to look down on the detective.

Lane shrugged. *Calling a lawyer will make you even later for your appointment. Stop wasting my time by establishing a pecking order.*

"Megan Newsome."

Lane got the distinct impression she thought the name should ring a bell with him, and it did. The Newsomes were regulars at his father's church. *I saw your face at my father's funeral.* He decided to wait for an answer to his initial question about the Randalls.

Megan sighed. "I didn't know them well. We travelled in different social circles. Met them at a charity event once and at the theatre last summer."

"Did you see anything unusual last night?"

Megan shook her head. "Not a thing. Are we finished?"

"For now." He stepped back, turned, and walked toward Nigel, who was tapping the face of his phone. "Get the plate?"

Nigel nodded. "Why? Did she lie to you?"

"I think so." Lane walked up the sidewalk and then the steps. Reaching the front door, he turning the knob and stepped inside. His nose was assaulted with the stench of blood, piss, bleach, and shit. Nigel closed the door behind them.

As he looked around the room, Lane spotted Dr. Colin Weaver, or Fibre, as Lane referred to him, head of the Forensic Crime Scene Unit. The doctor had the face and physique of a Michelangelo male on a Sistine ceiling, and the social skills of a shag carpet. *Let's hear what Fibre has to say.* Lane was one of the few who knew Fibre was the father of triplets. They lived with him and the extremely fertile PhD who'd seduced him and co-parented in the other half of Weaver's duplex. *And he's amazing with his kids.* Lane recalled seeing Fibre animated and smiling in the company of a trio of toddlers in the mall.

Weaver looked over his shoulder. He stood at the entrance to the living room. Lane noted the nine-foot ceiling was spattered with blood and brain matter.

"Hello, Detective," Weaver said.

"Can we take a look?" Lane asked.

Weaver nodded as he pulled back the hood on his white bunny suit. His blond hair stuck to his scalp. "Take a look if you like. Be careful, we're still working the scene." He used his right hand to wave them closer.

Lane and Nigel stepped under the curved opening in the wall. The corpses sat facing each other. Robert Randall was dressed in a black tuxedo. Elizabeth Randall wore a leather coat, a white blouse, and red pants. The back of Robert's head was visible, his chin on his chest. The exit wound was a pulpy mess of blood, bone, and tissue.

"It appears Mrs. Randall was shot in the mouth after witnessing the execution of her husband," Fibre said.

A chocolate-coloured Labrador retriever was crucified on a wall of birdseye maple, its sightless eyes staring at its masters.

It's all staged. The crucifixion of the family pet. The pair killed facing each other. The blood spatter on the ceiling. Whoever did this wants us to think it's art. Lane looked at the floor, seeing three round indentations in the carpet. *And the killer recorded it.*

Lane heard rapid breathing beside him and turned. Nigel's eyes were wide, staring at the scene.

His eyes aren't focused. Lane knew Nigel was reliving the horror of another scene.

Nigel's hands began to shake. He looked at them as if they belonged to someone else.

Lane looked back at Weaver. "Thank you. We've seen enough."

Lane grabbed Nigel at the elbow, got him turned around, opened the front door, and guided him down the front steps. He watched the cloud of frosty air puffing out of Nigel's open mouth. *He's hyperventilating.*

They made it to the Chev.

Lane opened the passenger door, got Nigel to climb inside, closed his door, and walked around the front of the car. He got in behind the wheel, closing his own door, and started the engine. Then he pulled the glove off of Nigel's left hand and handed it to him. "Breathe into your glove."

Nigel nodded, wide-eyed, placing the glove over his mouth. He exhaled. The fingers of the glove filled with air, imitating an open hand. Nigel inhaled. The fingers formed a fist.

Lane waited, watching Nigel's eyes as they began to focus. Nigel blinked, continuing to breathe into the glove.

What do I say to him?

Nigel closed his eyes and his chin dropped.

"You worked with Netsky?"

Nigel nodded.

"What was that like?"

Nigel took the glove away from his mouth. "He talked. I was supposed to listen."

"Then?"

"Netsky didn't like it when I asked questions."

Lane waited.

"He figured out I was smarter than he was. It pissed him off." Nigel put his hands over the dash where hot air was blasting onto the windshield. "Of course I didn't help the situation much. You know me. I understand that telling an unpleasant truth will piss people off, and I should keep my mouth shut. Then I say it anyway." He turned to smile at Lane.

"I need to ask this because we're partners."

"You want to know what happened in there?" Nigel asked.

Lane nodded.

"My father staged my mother's body. He had her sitting in a chair. Her eyes were wide open. Her head rested on her chin. The room had been cleaned with bleach. Some of the furniture had been turned over. He left the front door unlocked and said my mother must have done that. He made it appear as if an intruder had killed her. Then he went to work as if nothing had happened. Seeing the tableau in there brought it all back. Opening the door. Walking inside. Seeing the body of my mother. The stink of bleach." Nigel looked out of the window.

"You want off this case?"

"Are you fucking kidding? I want to hunt these assholes down!"

"How do you know it's more than one?" Lane asked.

"I assumed it would take two to subdue and record."

"Let's get to work, then. We need to review the files of the initial crime. Fibre will call us as soon as he has his preliminary findings." Lane shifted into drive, checking for traffic.

"How come you call him Fibre instead of Weaver or Colin?" Nigel asked.

"I don't know where the nickname came from. It's taken a few years, but I've come to understand he's more complicated than that."

"Aren't we all?"

×

"This is my case!" Fred Netsky stood across from Lane and looked sideways at Nigel. Fred was six four, weighed over two fifty, and was a year or two over forty. His hair was dyed black, styled and gelled to make him look younger.

Nigel opened his mouth, shutting it when Lane lifted his eyebrows.

"Hey, Freddy! Got your annuals seeded yet?" Lori wore her broad smile, new blue shoes, a blue pinstriped pantsuit, and glossy clear-coated nails.

Fred looked down at her. "I was planning on getting started in about a month."

"I don't know what you do to the soil, but those flowers of yours are amazing. Can't wait to see what you bring in this year." Lori looked up at Fred with frank admiration.

"The soil is my little secret." Fred smiled.

Lori blinked a couple of times to show off her blue eye shadow. "The detectives got their orders from the Chief. This case is theirs. You want me to get your old files?"

Fred shook his head. "I'll get them. I know where they are." He walked past Lori and down the hall.

Lori looked over her shoulder before stepping inside Lane's office. "Watch and learn, boys. If you want to survive around here, watch and learn."

chapter 2

"I phoned Alexandra. One of us will need to pick her up at the airport," Arthur said as Lane parked in the Foothills Medical Centre parking lot. "Christine really needs her sister with her."

Five minutes later, they stepped onto the elevator. Lane looked at Arthur while waiting for the door to close. Arthur's thinner face and hair made him appear younger. He smiled as he felt Lane's eyes on him.

Daniel's mother Lola led her husband John into the elevator. The brown-haired woman wore a pantsuit, a tasteful set of white pearls, a full-length cashmere coat, freshly dyed hair, and a frown aimed at Lane and Arthur. She turned her back on them to face the elevator door as it closed. Her husband John — dressed by Lola — was in a suit and peacoat to complement but not compete with his wife's outfit. He half-smiled at Lane and Arthur, turning his back when his wife took him by the elbow.

Lane watched the numbers light up above the door. *Dan's so different from his parents. Makes me wonder about genetic diversity.* Then he smiled. *Look at the family I came from.*

Arthur elbowed Lane in the ribs.

The door opened to the fifth floor, Lola exited first. Her heels click-clicked on the linoleum. John followed, then Lane and Arthur.

Arthur hummed. "Whatever Lola wants, Lola gets."

"You're forgetting Christine is a force of nature." Lane watched Lola and John as he pressed the button opening the electric doors to the ward. For a moment Lane was overcome by the desire to protect Christine and her baby. He began to move forward.

Arthur grabbed his arm. "Christine will ask for our help if she needs it. Let's just sit in the waiting room for a minute."

They sat in the chairs set along the hallway wall. As they got settled, Lane turned to observe the other family members waiting, sitting alongside and across. A grandmother with black hair wore an elaborate gold-and-bronze scarf. She stared at the metal doors. A man wearing a ball cap, a black leather jacket, and cowboy boots stared at his toes. His wife sat next to him reading a magazine.

"Stop that." Arthur put his hand on Lane's thigh.

Lane looked down to see his right knee bouncing.

The metal doors hummed open. Lane and Arthur turned when they heard the click-clicking of heels on the linoleum.

Lola swept through the opening. John ran to catch up.

"I was just explaining how she should breastfeed the child," Lola said.

"I know." John slowed to a fast walk.

"After all, I am a mother. I have considerable experience." Lola spotted Lane and Arthur before looking away.

Lane thought, *Didn't you hire nannies to look after your daughter and son?*

"She's a new mother. And her baby is in NICU," John said.

Lola stopped, facing her husband. "I hope you're not justifying her behaviour. She asked us to leave!"

"Just trying to explain." John took Lola by the elbow, heading for the elevator.

Lane and Arthur locked eyes as the sound of Lola's heels receded down the hallway.

A few minutes later, the metal doors opened again. Dan walked through and spied Lane and Arthur. "Would you like to meet my son?"

They followed him down the hallway, then through the NICU doors. They found a red-eyed Christine holding the baby. His hair was thick and black, his eyes were closed, and an IV nestled in a vein in his forehead.

What is going on? Lane took a closer look at Christine. She wore a white housecoat. Her hair was tied back. Besides being exhausted, she looked defeated.

Dan said, "He's on antibiotics to prevent infection."

Arthur cupped his hand over the back of the baby's head. Christine smiled.

"He's beautiful," Arthur said.

"We'll probably be out in a few days," Dan said.

He can't stop talking, Lane thought.

Christine looked up at Lane. "Do you think I'll be a good mom?"

Dan stood up. "My mother was just here." He held his hands out with the palms up, shrugging.

"She said a good mother knows how to breastfeed instinctively," Christine said.

Lane sat down next to Christine. She passed the baby over.

Lane felt the warm weight of the newborn, looked at the soft tan of his face.

"His name is Indiana," Dan said.

Arthur said, "You know, I've been talking with Loraine and Lisa." Loraine and Lisa, old friends of Lane and Arthur, had a son named Ben.

Christine leaned forward, focusing on Arthur.

Lane touched the delicate skin of Indiana's cheek.

Arthur said, "They said it took a day or two for Ben to learn to latch on to the breast. That mother and son had to learn together."

"Really?" Christine asked.

Arthur nodded.

Lane smiled at the baby.

Indiana farted.

Arthur smiled. "See? He's already learning to communicate."

×

Lane opened the passenger door of their BMW. It smelled of soft leather and new carpet. Arthur sat in the driver's seat. "If Lola thinks she can treat Christine like that, it won't only be Christine who's giving her the boot. *Kharra alhika!* She struts around in her 'look at me, notice me' shoes with her whipped husband trotting along behind. She thinks being aggressive gets her what she wants, and we'll all roll over like beaten dogs."

Lane stepped out into the sharp bite of minus twenty air and closed the door quickly. He could hear Arthur swearing in Arabic over the sound of the heater fan and the engine as he walked behind the car. He crossed the street and walked up the ramp to the Crowfoot LRT station. *At least he's over being depressed. Now he's ready to take on anyone and everyone.* He walked along the bridge over Crowchild Trail. Below him a steady stream of traffic pushed through the heavy arctic air. Exhaust trailed in white plumes.

The north wind bit the back of his neck, and he pulled up the collar of his winter jacket. Ahead, the curved metal-and-glass station looked like the back end of an ocean wave. He stepped inside, bathed by a blast of warm air.

Twenty minutes later, he stepped off the LRT and walked across 7th Avenue, down the block into the teeth of the wind funneling between the buildings, and into the sand-coloured concrete building housing the Calgary Police Service.

He unzipped his jacket and took off his black cap.

Lori greeted him as he entered the office. She wore a red suit jacket, a white scarf and blouse, and black slacks. "How's that new baby?"

He smiled. "Perfect. He's got a head full of black hair. His skin is so soft."

Lori said, "So he's turned you into a real softy?"

Lane frowned. "I guess he has."

"Don't worry. It suits you."

"What's new around here?" Lane put his cap and gloves on the countertop, shucking off his winter jacket.

Lori leaned forward, dropping her voice to a whisper. "Fred Netsky has been wandering around trying to play the victim since the Chief gave you his old case. But so far, no one is biting. In fact, the others are beginning to avoid him. Looks like they're adopting a wait-and-see policy since you're the boss around here."

Lane nodded. "Thanks." Then he went inside his office, hanging his coat and hat behind the door. *What was I doing when Byron Thomas was arrested?*

Lane looked at the date on the file in front of him. *That was at the height of Chief Smoke's reign. I was persona non grata around here. The only person who would speak with me or make eye contact was Lori. Things sure have changed. Now the detectives answer to me.*

He looked more closely at the file. The evidence was straightforward. Byron Thomas was found a couple of blocks from the scene. The victims' blood was found in the treads of his right shoe. Jewellery from a separate robbery was in his pockets. His voice was a match to the 911 call made fifteen minutes earlier. After questioning, Byron confessed to the murders.

Lane read on, spotting an inconsistency in the times of death. The coroner's report said the victims died at least four hours before Thomas' 911 call.

Lori opened the door, looking at Nigel's empty desk. "There's a call for you. Someone claiming to be your sister. Says her name is Alison."

Lane frowned, feeling his stomach begin a slow aerobatic manoeuvre. "Thanks for the heads up."

Lori closed the door. A few seconds later his phone rang. He took a couple of slow breaths before picking it up.

"Paul?" Alison asked.

"How are you?" Lane asked.

"Is it true?" she asked.

She's wound up tighter than last time she called. Was that three years ago, or four? "Is what true?" Lane asked.

"Did Christine have a baby boy?"

Lane heard the sarcasm in her tone. "Yes."

"And you think I will allow you to turn my grandson gay?"

Lane wasn't sure if he reacted to the sanctimony, the ignorance, or the sarcasm. He was sure he felt a breach in a dam holding back years of resentment at the way he'd been judged then abandoned by members of his family. Emotions began to overwhelm his self-control. He took a long breath to help him channel the overpowering emotions. "You mean the child of the daughter you abandoned?"

Alison inhaled sharply.

Go for it! "The daughter you excommunicated? If memory serves, you didn't even bother to get out of the van. Wasn't that visit squeezed in between trips to shopping malls?"

"YOU DARE JUDGE ME?"

Lane moved the phone away from his ear, but kept his mouth close. "How dare you call me with your phony concern for a grandson after you abandoned your daughter? How many years has it been?"

"It was for her own good. God spoke to me. He told me what needed to be done!"

Just another zealot, like John A. Jones, who blew himself up with his own bomb. "How can you say God told you it was for her own good?"

"Because God knows!" Alison said.

"God knows you abandoned your daughter. God knows you signed over legal guardianship to Arthur and me." *Why are you baiting her?*

"God knows!" she said.

Enough of this. "What do you want?"

"My lawyer is going to take my grandchild away from you. The child needs protection from you and your Arthur."

He heard her tone of triumph. "That's funny, because you and your husband claimed you couldn't afford to pay your legal bills when Paradise was investigated for polygamy and tax evasion. Were you lying for the Lord?"

"How did you know about that?" Alison said.

"The lying or the money?" Lane stared at the phone, feeling an overwhelming weariness.

"God knows that my grandson needs my protection!"

Give it a rest, Alison. "What is your grandson's name?"

Another abrupt inhalation from Alison.

"Christine has just had a baby boy. If you threaten her or the child in any way, you will have to go through me first."

"I have rights! I am the grandmother! I will get a lawyer!"

"Go ahead. Get a lawyer." Lane waited for her reaction. *Just hang up. No, you've got to let her focus her anger on you instead of Christine.*

"I'm going to pray. God will tell me what to do." Alison hung up.

Lane felt something akin to relief at finally saying what he'd wanted to say to his sister. Then he dialed the office of his lawyer, Tommy Pham.

×

"I don't get it," Lane said.

"What don't you get?" Arthur sat across from him at their kitchen table. It was made of maple and had gathered an assortment of artifacts: an unused diaper, a letter addressed to Matt, a battery, a coffee cup, two light bulbs, three plates, a salad bowl.

The scent of salmon cooked with butter, maple syrup, and lemon juice filled the kitchen. Lane picked a piece of cucumber from the salad bowl, holding it in front of his mouth. "I don't get the fact that I don't hear from Alison for — what is it, three or four years? — and then she calls and goes crazy."

"In Alison's mind, Christine was supposed to be punished." Arthur popped a forkful of salmon in his mouth. He looked at Sam, who sat next to him with an expression suggesting he hoped a morsel or two would come his way. Roz, their older dog, reclined on the throw rug in front of the sink.

"It's crazy. The kid left Paradise. She was excommunicated. She's supposed to be punished for the rest of her life?" Lane used a large spoon to put some salad on his plate.

"*You're* supposed to be punished for the rest of your life." Arthur covered his mouth, pointing his fork at his partner. "You were excommunicated from your family. You were supposed to be miserable without them. They probably expected you to have an epiphany and come back straight. You didn't, so in their minds you continue to need to be punished. Why should Christine be any different?"

Lane shook his head. "This is fucked up."

Arthur chuckled. "Now you get to see Indiana and Alison doesn't. He's her grandson, and you haven't seen the light, changed your wicked lifestyle, left me. In her mind —" he pointed the fork at Lane and then at himself "— we're the ones who're fucked up."

"But we're no threat to anyone. Why is she so threatened?" Lane poured dressing on the fresh greens.

"There's a new leader in Paradise. Your sister no longer has the influence she once had."

Lane shrugged. "Who told you this?"

"Christine. She still talks with some of the people who live or once lived in Paradise. The power Alison used to have is fading. Apparently she married this new guy named Milton after the other guy died of a heart attack. The younger wives have Milton's ear. Now Alison finds out she has a grandson she can't see, and she's angry at you because your life is better than hers." Arthur put another forkful of salmon in his mouth.

Lane shook his head. *It doesn't make sense. It's not going to make sense. You're upset because it's your sister, you came from the same parents, you grew up in the same house, and you still don't understand the way she thinks. The situation is not going to change, so you might as well think about something else.* "Where's Matt?"

"He insisted on picking up Alex at the airport."

"I forgot. Alex gets in at what time?" Lane thought about how Christine would react to the arrival of her half-sister who shared the same father.

"She landed about two hours ago."

"Where are they?" Lane looked out the window, seeing a cloud of white rising from the chimney of the neighbour's furnace.

Arthur shook his head. "Alex is an aunt for the first time."

"They're at the hospital."

"And she's catching up with her sister," Arthur said.

"They won't be home any time soon, then."

"Exactly."

×

The front door opened and winter air flowed down the stairs. Lane felt the cold lick his ankles as they watched TV. Something heavy thumped the floor above them.

"I forgot. This is Canada. I have to take my boots off at the front door." The voice was female with a slight Boston accent.

"It's Alex!" Arthur threw off his comforter, sitting up on the couch. Lane stood up.

Sam yawned. Roz barked. Arthur followed Lane to the foot of the stairs.

Alex stood at the top, put her hand on the railing, and stepped down.

She looks like a Cossack princess. She was wearing a full-length grey Russian military coat with a double row of polished gold buttons. On her head, she wore a round faux-fur hat.

Alex floated down the stairs then embraced each of them.

Lane caught the scent of Jean Patou's Joy. *Only the best for you, girl.*

"Hold me close, boys, this girl hasn't been warm since she left the States!" Alex undid her coat. Matt took it for her, waiting for the hat. Alex flipped her hat over her shoulder without a backward glance, stepping into the centre of the room. Lane watched Matt retreat upstairs to the closet with Alex's coat and hat.

Alex sat down in front of the gas fireplace, gathering her black skirt and tucking it between her legs. "Who is this handsome fellow?" Alex pointed at Sam, who was rolling on his back, his front legs pawing the air, his rear legs splayed.

"That's Sam." Matt reached the bottom step, sitting in the chair next to Lane. Alex rubbed Sam under the chin.

"Sam!" Matt stood up.

"That boy's got his lipstick out." Alex pulled her hand away. Matt shooed Sam upstairs.

"Isn't my nephew the most gorgeous little man you've ever seen in your life?" Alex spread her arms, her black hair backlit by the fire.

She could be Christine's twin. Well, if Christine were as much of a dame as Alex.

"We think he's perfect." Arthur pointed at Lane and Matt.

"He is that." Alex leaned back, closing her eyes.

Lane saw the way Matt watched Alex and was oblivious to all else. *Oh no!*

chapter 3

"Anything new?" Lane stepped into the office.

Nigel's face glowed blue against the reflected light of the computer screen.

Lane took off his winter jacket, tucking his black gloves into the sleeves before hanging it up. As he turned he saw Nigel frown, then lean back, reaching forward with his hands, tilting upright, tucking his head forward, and locking his fingers behind his head.

The knuckles are red. He's been boxing again. Lane stood across from his partner and waited.

"The Randalls' son and daughter are coming in tomorrow morning for an interview." Nigel looked at the ceiling.

"What's up?" Lane stepped closer to Nigel's desk.

Nigel made eye contact. Lane almost recoiled at the intensity of Nigel's rage.

"I've been doing some research." Nigel looked to the right. Lane waited.

"There's a series of similar events." Nigel made eye contact again.

Lane stood still. *This case is becoming a nightmare.*

Nigel looked at the door. Lane turned and closed it.

"Netsky fucked up." Nigel said it so matter-of-factly, and with such vehemence, it landed like a punch.

Lane sat in his chair, turning to face Nigel. "Explain."

Nigel pointed at his computer screen. "I've done a cursory search on two databases. Approximately six months after the initial murder, there was a similar event in Toronto. Then six months after that, one in New York. And another in Playa del Carmen."

"Where was the last one?"

Nigel frowned. "Mexican Riviera. Lots of Canadians holiday there in the winter."

"So there have been four similar murders since Byron Thomas was convicted?"

Nigel nodded. "So far."

Lane stared at the door. *I remember the one in Mexico. It became a big story here. They arrested a local who killed himself in prison.* "Any of them solved?"

"Just the one in Mexico." Nigel rolled his eyes.

"Sensitive about tourism dollars?"

"Maybe. It's hard for people up here to understand how it works down there."

Lane waited and, when Nigel said no more, asked, "How does it work down there?"

Nigel looked into the distance within the room. "Part of it is about the belief *fresas* can afford it, so it's okay to rip them off."

"Fresas?"

"Strawberries. Wealthy, snobby, elitist, entitled tourists."

"And?"

"Part of it is survival. Lots of jobs depend on a safe place for fresas to spend their money and support the local economy. Families go hungry if the tourists stop coming."

"And investors lose money."

Nigel nodded. "The same as here. People in power want to protect their money. There, the corruption is systemic, especially in the way many of the police operate. It creates an environment where justice is quick on the draw but often off the mark."

"So it looks like maybe they found a patsy."

"Just like we did."

"Exactly." *And because we didn't get it right the first time, more people are dead.*

Nigel pointed at his computer screen. "There's another interesting bit of information."

"Okay."

"Each of the dead couples has a residence in Calgary."

"Any more connections?" Lane asked.

"That's it so far except, of course, for the fact that all of the victims were well off."

"You keep gathering up the details until we hear from Fibre." He got up, walked to the door, opened it, and poked his head out.

Lori sat at her desk. She turned to face him with a nail file in her right hand.

"Do you still have a contact at WestJet?" he asked.

Lori nodded, continuing to run the file over her nails. "No time to say *good morning?*"

Lane smiled.

"I'll call Angela. You gonna get the paperwork rolling?" Lori finished her nails and set the file down.

"Nigel will get the dates to you, and I will get the paperwork for Angela."

Lori picked up the phone with her right hand, dismissing him with her left. "Go on. I can do this without some big strong detective looking over my shoulder."

Lane went back inside his office, noting Nigel's smile, and got down to work.

I'm standing in front of the scene of Calgary's latest homicide, discovered on Monday morning. Robert and Elizabeth Randall have now been identified as the couple found murdered in their home.

The Calgary Police Service has released no other details about the victims except to say the investigation is ongoing.

Robert Randall and his wife Elizabeth were well respected in the Calgary arts community. The couple shied away from the limelight but were strong supporters of various charities and initiatives in Calgary.

CUT TO JANE MANN, CALGARY ARTS COUNCIL "The Randalls were such lovely people. [pause] They gave generously to so many causes. Their loss is a tragedy, and they will be deeply missed."

The surviving members of the Randall family have asked for privacy as they make funeral arrangements.

This is the fifth murder of a prominent Calgarian couple in the last three years.

Shazia Wajdan, CBC News, Calgary.

"He latched on right away this morning." Christine sat in a chair next to Indiana's crib. The IV stand supported a blue machine dispensing antibiotics. The medicine came from a clear plastic bag, snaking through a tube and ending in the needle entering the vein in the baby's forehead. She adjusted the blanket draped over her shoulder, covering her breast and Indy's face.

Lane looked at Indiana's feet, noticing the boy had his ankles crossed. He reached out, touching the arch of Indiana's foot with his index finger. He heard the sounds of a satisfied baby sucking at his mother's breast and Indiana breathing through his nose.

"How is Lori?" Christine asked.

"She chased me out of the office to come and see you."

Christine smiled, lifting the blanket to watch her son. Lane saw the transformation from young woman to mother in the way her eyes softened. Christine looked at her uncle. He saw the protective instinct sharpen her focus when she looked over his shoulder.

Lane heard a pair of notice-me heels.

"Lola's back." Christine held Indiana closer.

Lane stood and turned.

"Oh, hello." Lola took off her cashmere coat, setting it over the head of Indiana's crib.

"Don't hang it there. I'm worried about infection," Christine said.

There was a sharp intake of breath. Lola's face reddened as she lifted the coat and held it draped over her arms. "How's he doing?"

"Better," Christine said.

"Can I hold him?"

"He's hungry, and my uncle was here first." Christine adjusted something under the blanket.

Lola looked at Lane, opened her mouth to protest, thought better of it, and closed her lips.

Wow, didn't think I'd ever see that.

Christine sat up straighter, her eyes growing hard as she looked past her uncle.

Lane turned to see a woman wearing a long grey nylon winter coat. Her yellow dress reached the tops of her black winter boots. Her coat was open, and the ruffles of her dress covered her neck. Her hair was long and greying, snaking around her shoulder in a braided rope, falling over one breast, and reaching below her navel. Beside her stood a girl of maybe fourteen whose brown, wiry hair sprang out in an unruly fro. Her eyes were brown and bright, but the rest of her face was a mask. She wore a dress of the same material and style as the other woman. Her eyes lifted from the floor to study Christine.

"Hello, Sarah." Christine said.

Indiana sighed.

They watched as Christine adjusted her left breast under the cover of the blanket, then tucked the blanket around the baby so they could see his sleeping face and thick black hair.

The woman with the braided hair took a step closer.

Lane saw fear in Christine's eyes and moved to position himself between the women and his niece. He looked around at the babies who occupied nearby cribs.

"You don't even recognize your own sister, Pauline?" The woman with the braid took another step closer.

The contempt in the woman's voice slapped Lane out of his daze. "What do you want, Alison?"

"My grandson, of course. I'm here to meet him and hold him."

Lola moved to stand shoulder to shoulder with Lane. He sensed Christine standing up. He could hear her palm tapping Indiana on the back. Indy burped. A machine whirred.

"Move out of my way," Alison continued. "I need to see my grandson."

Christine said, "A pickup truck will be downstairs with Milton or one of his bishops at the wheel waiting for my mother and the baby."

Lane saw a nurse approaching. *If anything starts in here, there's a very good chance one of these babies will be hurt.* He leaned his head to the left, making eye contact with the nurse. "Call security, please."

The nurse went to a phone on the wall, lifting it from its cradle.

Alison looked over her shoulder. Sarah looked at the floor.

Alison turned back to face them. "God told me to raise this child."

Lane shook his head.

Lola said, "Well, then, you can just tell God this child belongs with his mother."

Alison took a sharp, short breath. "Who are you?" Alison tried to look around the pair standing between her and her objective.

"Indiana's other grandmother." Lola stood with feet apart.

"Then you understand it's best for the child to be away from Pauline." She pointed at Lane.

Lola kept her voice low, but Lane heard the threat. "I like to make up my own mind about things, and I've learned Christine is the same way."

Lane saw a man enter the NICU. He was over six foot six. He wore a blue winter jacket, a green baseball cap, a frown, and the smell of the country.

Lane looked at the nurse who stood by the phone. He turned to Christine. "You holding Indy close?"

Christine said, "Damn right."

Lane turned to Alison. "This is called child abduction." He spotted the nurse hanging up the phone.

"God knows what kind of man you are, Pauline!" Alison's eyes were wide. Sarah took a step back, looking at the exit sign.

The speaker in the hallway announced, "Code amber in NICU! Code amber in NICU!"

The man in the green baseball cap looked at Alison.

Lane looked past them, noting the room was filling with nurses. A woman in a black uniform sidled to the front of the crowd. She was about five and a half feet tall and appeared to be about three feet wide. Her black hair was tied back, and she wore Kevlar gloves. The white reflective labels on either side of her Kevlar vest read *Security* and *Scott*.

Dan arrived with four cups of coffee. His eyes opened wide. He positioned himself where he could see Christine and the baby. Then his eyes locked on the back of the big man with the green hat.

The man in the green hat turned to Scott. "We're leaving with the child."

Scott leaned sideways, looking at Christine. "You the mother?"

Dan set down the coffees on a tray, moving closer to the man with the green hat. Christine nodded.

Scott pointed at the man in the green hat. "Is he supposed to be here?"

Christine shook her head.

Scott took a step closer to the man in the green hat. "Come with me, sir."

"He will not," Alison said.

Scott looked at Christine, who said, "They want to take my baby." Scott grabbed Alison by the elbow. Alison shook the guard off.

The man in the green hat reached for Scott. She took him by the wrist, snapping it back against his forearm. He yelped, falling to his knees.

Alison took a swing at Scott, who ducked the blow. A pair of nurses grabbed Alison by the elbows, dragging her out of NICU. The heels of Alison's winter boots squealed across the floor. "That is my grandson! God wants him to be with me! God told me!"

A baby in a nearby crib began to scream. A nurse rushed to attend to the infant.

Lane looked over his shoulder at Christine, who was staring down at Indy and wiping her tears with the blanket. She began to sob. Dan moved closer, putting his arm around her shoulders.

Lola turned to Lane. "Is your family always this entertaining?"

✕

"Your sister is fucking crazy." Matt looked at Lane from where he sat in front of the TV with the sound muted. An NFL game was on.

"And now she's in jail?" Alex asked.

"Four people were arrested, including the one waiting outside in the truck." Lane looked at the screen, watching the players line up on either side of the football.

"What about Sarah?" Arthur rubbed Sam behind the ear. The dog smiled.

"She was released after my brother Joseph came down and took her to his place. She explained the plan was to take Indiana to a fundamentalist compound in the Utah desert." The centre moved, the quarterback stepping back ready to pass. "I got a chance to talk with her. She seems very nice. Very quiet, but she did ask a couple of questions about Christine."

The quarterback was blind-sided by a linebacker. Both players pounded the turf.

Matt said, "That's gotta hurt. What kinds of questions?"

"Yes," Arthur asked, "what kinds of questions?"

"Like where Christine went to school, if she was still going to school with the baby, what Dan was like, and how long she's been living with us."

Arthur pushed Sam to the side. "Not our address and phone number so they can come after Indiana again when they get out of jail?"

Lane shook his head. "Most of the questions were about school."

Arthur leaned forward. "After what happened to Matt and Jessica, this has me worried all over again."

Matt shook his head. "We've handled this kind of thing before, and we'll handle it again. We need to talk with Dan and work out the details, that's all." He got up, taking a deep breath.

He's having a flashback of when he and Jessica were taken.

"Details?" Alex asked.

"A plan. Dr. Alexandre told me to always have a plan to cope with the PTSD." Matt tapped the side of his head with a finger. "I'm working on the details."

Arthur glanced at Lane. "Let's hear what you've got so far."

Matt watched the TV. A player the size of a major appliance was helping the quarterback to his feet. "First we need to agree there will always be two of us with Indiana at all times. Then we need to have communications." He turned to Lane. "Do we still have those fancy phones?"

"I can get them." Lane nodded.

Matt pointed at Arthur. "Can you program them again?"

Arthur said, "Sure."

Matt turned to Lane. "Then we need a backup. Does Harper know what happened with your sister and Milton, and their plan to take Indy to Utah?"

Lane stood. "I'll call him to make sure he's aware so he can handle details from his end. He needs to know Daniel, Christine, and Indiana have been transferred to a secure room at the Children's Hospital." *Here we go again.* "This time we'll stay a step or two ahead of the game."

chapter 4

David and Melissa Randall stared vacantly at the grey conference-room wall.

Lane looked for signs of grief. Both looked exhausted. Their bodies sagged in their chairs. Rapid weight loss was sketched on their faces. And there was rage underneath it.

Melissa Randall stood about five foot six and looked at Lane as if challenging him. She tucked her greying black hair behind her ears. David Randall, her brother, was closer to six feet tall. When he took off his black winter coat, Lane could see his scalp beneath thinning black hair. Both looked to be in their late thirties.

"I'm Detective Lane." He gestured with his right hand. "This is Detective Li."

"What do you want?" Melissa eyed them warily. David tried to smile. Melissa hooked her thumb in David's direction. "We've done some research online. My parents weren't the first."

David nodded. "The newspaper says our parents are the fifth victims. Some homeless guy named Byron Thomas was convicted for a similar crime. After what happened to Mom and Dad, do you think maybe Thomas is innocent?"

Lane inhaled. He saw Nigel open his mouth. *Oh no! Nigel, tread lightly.*

Nigel tapped his file. "Actually there may be more than five crimes attributable to the same killers. I've been tracking a series of murders with similar characteristics."

Melissa looked at her brother. David said, "This isn't what we expected."

"What did you expect?"

Melissa pointed at the detectives. "That you would be covering your asses."

Nigel said, "We'd like to put the killers' asses in a cell."

David put his arm around Melissa's shoulders. "What can we do to help?"

Lane asked, "Do you have any thoughts about who might want to harm your parents?"

Melissa shook her head. "Besides Mom's crazy sister, I have no idea."

Lane lifted his eyebrows.

David said, "Our mom has a sister named Peggy who was always trying to get Dad into the sack, because her husband was sterile. Then her husband died, and she got even crazier. Dad told some people at a party he was tired of Peggy trying to get into his pants. The story got back to her, and she denied it. Then she made a number of threats. We've learned to ignore her."

Lane looked at Nigel, who had painted an impassive expression on his face. His eyes, however, were lit with mischief.

"Peggy's last name?" Lane asked.

"Carr." Melissa used her finger to indicate she wanted Lane's pen. He handed it over with some paper. Melissa pulled out a smart phone, scrolled through some numbers, wrote one down, then slid paper and pen back to Lane's side of the table.

"Have your parents had any recent gatherings at their house?" Nigel asked.

David and Melissa looked at each other. David turned to Nigel. "They had their annual get-together. It was an after-New Year's party. January eleventh, I think it was."

"Is there any way we could get a guest list?" Nigel asked.

What angle is Nigel working on? Lane wondered.

"Why do you need a guest list?" Melissa asked.

You are definitely experiencing the anger stage of the grieving process.

Nigel looked at Lane.

So you step in the shit and want me to clean your shoes? Lane turned his palms face up. "Because this is the early stage of the investigation, we have to look at a variety of avenues." *Nigel, next time let me know your angle before the interview.*

"Sounds like bullshit to me." Melissa glared at Lane.

Nigel tapped the table with his forefinger. "In earlier killings the couples were murdered within a month of having a social gathering in their homes. The killers took valuable items and cash. We're trying to establish whether or not your parents may have been victims of serial killers."

Shit!

Melissa looked at Lane. "That wasn't so hard, now, was it? Hand over the paper and pen, and we'll put our heads together."

Five minutes later, David and Melissa had a list of close to forty names, some with phone numbers, a few with business titles. David pushed the list across the table to Lane. "What else do you need?"

Lane slid the list to Nigel, who said, "I want to do some cross checking." He stood up and left the room.

Lane stared at the open door, then turned to the brother and sister.

Melissa looked at her watch. "We've got a meeting with a funeral director in an hour."

Lane asked, "When will the funeral be?"

"Saturday." David looked at his sister. Melissa nodded.

"I'd like to attend if you don't mind." Lane studied their reactions.

David shrugged. Melissa said, "Knock yourself out. The service is at two."

Lane took a breath. "What are the best numbers for us to get in touch with you?"

Melissa stood up, walked around the table, picked up Lane's pen, and wrote down two numbers. She put her name next to one and David's next to another. Lane caught the scent of strawberry from her shampoo. He watched as Melissa walked out the conference door followed by her brother.

Lane looked at the sheet of paper, pulled out his cell phone, and entered the numbers. Then he walked to his office, closed the door, and sat at his desk.

Nigel's fingers were dancing over the keyboard.

Lane asked, "Why the question about the guest list?"

The tone of Lane's voice made Nigel's head snap back. Then his wide eyes focused on his partner. "I've been looking over Netsky's files, and I've had e-mails from officers investigating two of the other murders. In both cases the victims had major social events at their homes less than a month before the murders. It was one thought I had."

"Let me in on your plans the next time," Lane said, then added, "please."

Nigel blushed. "I thought..."

"We're a team?"

Nigel nodded.

"Then we both need to be on the same page." Lane looked at his computer. "What do you plan to do with the guest list?"

Nigel had his hands hovering over the keyboard. "Cross-reference it with the passenger lists of flights from Toronto, New York, and Cancun a week before and a week after the murders."

Lane nodded. "Good work." He turned to his computer to map out the various bits of the investigation using a program called Inspirations. He added crime-scene photos where necessary.

An hour later Nigel pushed his chair back. "Want a mocha-ccino?"

Lane nodded. "Please." He reached into his shirt pocket for a bill.

"I got it." Nigel walked out the door.

Five minutes later, Lori walked into Lane's office, closing the door behind her. "What did you do to Nigel?"

Lane looked at her as she stood across from him, her fists on the hips of her black dress. "Just get your nails done?"

Lori lifted her right hand, looking at her red nails and smiling. "Don't change the subject."

"What did he say to you?"

Lori cocked her head to the right. "Not a damned thing! It was the expression on his face that gave him away."

"I asked him to keep me better informed before we do our next interview. Sometimes he forgets we're a team." Lane felt his face redden.

"Do you know the kid has been picking up the slack for you because you're busy with the new baby?" Lori put her fists on Lane's desk. Her posture revealed her ample cleavage.

"I didn't know." Lane leaned forward. *You want to fight? Let's fight!*

"Do you know Netsky's been whining about you taking on this investigation? It's obvious he thinks he fucked up on his end, and he's trying to make the shit stick to you. Nigel has been running interference for you and countering Netsky's bullshit with facts." Lori stood up, crossing her arms under her breasts.

"I didn't know that." Lane sat back in his chair and exhaled. *But it's to be expected.*

"Now you know." Lori looked over her shoulder. "When do I get to see some pictures of this new baby?"

Lane picked up his cell phone, found the photos, and handed the phone to Lori.

"He looks like you, apart from the fact that he has more hair."

Lane laughed. "I don't know who he looks like, but he sure does have lots of hair."

The meaty side of a fist pounded Lane's office door. It startled Lori, who launched the cell phone into the air. She managed to catch it with her fingertips before it hit the floor.

Lane opened the door. Harper stood there, red faced. "What the hell is your sister up to?"

Lane felt Lori's eyes on him. "My sister and her—what do you call Milton if he has multiple wives? Spouse? Anyway, we took care of it and now Christine, the baby, and Dan are all safe. Alison, Milton, and some guy named Pratt are in jail."

"Someone tried to take Indiana?" Lori looked from Lane to Harper, who moved deeper into the office.

"Someone tried to take your baby?" Nigel stood in the open doorway with a cardboard tray of coffee and tea.

"My sister —" Lane started to explain all over again.

"— must be absofuckinlutely out of her mind." Nigel moved past Harper, handing a coffee to Lane, a tea to Lori, and another cup to Harper.

Harper took the cup from Nigel. "Where's yours?"

"He gave it to you," Lori said.

Harper went to hand the coffee back.

Nigel put his hands in the air. "It's all good." He turned to Lane. "How come you didn't tell us about the baby?"

"The baby is fine. We stopped them from getting close to Indiana." Lane took a sip of mochaccino, noting the people in the room were eyeing him with expressions ranging from disbelief to cut the bullshit.

"'We'?" Harper asked.

Lane took the cup away from his mouth. "Dan's mother was there."

"Lola?" Lori asked.

Lane nodded.

"The two of you stopped them?" Harper took a sip of coffee. Evidently liking what he tasted, he looked at the cup and took another sip.

"Actually a security guard stepped in and took down Pratt. A couple of nurses took care of Alison. And Lola, Dan, and I were between the crazies and the baby." Lane looked at the faces of his colleagues.

"So you didn't bother to mention this to any of us because...?" Lori asked.

How do I answer that one? Lane took another sip of coffee instead.

"Good thing you didn't try to talk your way out of that one." Harper pointed his coffee at Lane.

"I've got some names here." Nigel pointed at his computer screen.

Lane looked at Nigel, and for an instant they connected. Lane thought, *You're changing the subject to get me out of this mess.*

"I'll print out the list. There are four people on both the party list and the airline passenger lists. We've got some work to do." Nigel pressed a button, heading out the door to retrieve the list from Lori's printer.

Lori pointed a manicured finger at Lane, smiling. "Do you need to be reminded we are a team in this office?"

I had that coming.

×

It took Lane fifteen minutes to find Indiana's hospital room. It was hidden within the red, yellow, and blue Lego architecture of the Children's Hospital. He knocked on the door. Dan opened it while holding a finger to his lips. He pointed at Indiana asleep in the crib, and Christine asleep on a bed near the window. Dan stepped into the hallway, carefully closing the door.

"How are they doing?" Lane smelled sweat and unwashed clothes.

"Christine is afraid her mom or somebody else from Paradise will show up to steal Indiana." Dan looked down the hall as a woman approached with flowers, then stepped into a nearby room. A security guard poked his head out from around a wall next to the nursing station. Dan nodded and waved.

"Why don't you take a break? Get something to eat. I'll stay here and keep an eye on things while you're gone." Lane took his winter jacket off.

Dan looked at the door, frowning.

"Go on. I'll be here. Take a break."

Dan smiled, turned, and walked down the hall. Lane saw the exhaustion curving across his shoulders and down his spine.

Lane opened the door, closed it, and hung his coat on the chair. The breathing of the baby pulled him closer to the crib. He leaned against the top rail, watching the rise and fall of Indy's chest. He listened for each inhale and exhale. He listened for the door. Time passed. He heard Christine sit up. Lane turned toward his niece and saw her smile. "He's beautiful, isn't he?"

Lane nodded, unable to speak.

"Uncle Arthur was up earlier with Matt."

He nodded again.

"And Lola just left. She helped protect us yesterday, didn't she?" Christine got up, stuffing her feet into a pair of pink slippers. She wore a red T-shirt and black pajama bottoms.

"She did." Lane wanted to touch Indy's cheek but was afraid of waking him.

"It's good to have family standing up for you, isn't it?"

Lane nodded. "It is."

She put her arm around his shoulder, leaning her head against his neck.

chapter 5

"What have you got?" Lane set a coffee down on Nigel's desk, sipping from his own cup.

Nigel looked up, puzzled, and took the cup. "I'm trying to understand the connections between the lists. There are some. They just don't make any sense."

"What doesn't make sense?" Lane looked over Nigel's shoulder at the computer screen, frowning at the layers of open windows of data on his screen. "Send it over to me bit by bit. I'll divide it into manageable portions." He went to his desk, sat down, and double clicked on an icon.

Five hours later, Lori opened the door. "Aren't you two going for lunch?"

Nigel looked up at her. "Do you know how we can get one of those big monitors?"

Lori lifted her chin as Lane looked up from his small monitor. She said, "Give me a couple of minutes."

Thirty minutes later, one of the department's tech specialists knocked. Nigel opened the door. She wore a black blouse and slacks, a pair of pumps, and a tool belt.

The black-haired woman had an exotic accent, rolling her Rs. "You ordered a bigger monitor?"

Lane nodded. "That's right."

She pointed at them. "Give me a hand with this new one, then get out of my way."

"Who are you?" Nigel asked.

"Nebal. Lori sent me." She put her fists on her hips, pursing her red lips.

Lane saved what they'd been working on. "Want me to shut my computer down?"

Nebal nodded, moving into the office. She stood behind Lane's monitor, watching as he shut down. When the computer's cooling fan slowed, she disconnected the monitor.

Nigel and Lane picked up the new black-framed monitor from the flatbed cart in the hallway, manoeuvring it into the office. Nebal eased past them as she took the old monitor out. She smelled of incense. The detectives set the new monitor on Lane's desk. It came within centimetres of spanning from one corner of the desk to the other.

Lori stood in the doorway. "Nebal, have you met these two before?" The tech stood up from behind the new monitor.

Lane turned, seeing Netsky looking over the top of Lori's head. The detective glared as he took in the scene. "New toy?" There was sarcasm in his tone.

Lori turned. "Haven't you got work to do, big boy?"

Netsky moved on down the hallway.

Lori turned back to face the men and pointed. "This is Detective Lane, and this is Detective Li." She pointed at the tech. "This is Nebal."

"How did you make this happen so fast?" Lane asked.

Lori gave Lane one of her you–don't–really–want–to–know looks. "Get out of here and get some lunch so she can do her job."

Lane and Nigel grabbed their winter coats and made their way outside. The sun sat low in the western sky, reflecting off the snow and making them reach for sunglasses as they walked west down the Stephen Avenue Mall toward the Greasy Spoon, a restaurant that never lived up to its name. A breeze blew down the mall, turning exposed flesh white and carrying their frosty breath away.

Nigel opened the door to the Greasy Spoon. They stepped inside, greeted by a blast of warm air and a curtain separating patrons from the cold.

A dark-haired waitress spotted them. Lane held up two fingers. "This way," the waitress said, leading them past the counter and up the stairs to a table. "Coffee?"

"Please." Lane took his jacket off, stuffing mitts and cap into the sleeve and hanging it on the back of his chair.

Nigel sat down across from him. The waitress returned with menus and a carafe of coffee. Both detectives stared at the steaming black liquid filling their cups. Neither spoke until the coffee had been doctored with cream and sugar and the first few sips of the narcotic's warmth began to work its magic.

"I don't think like you do." Nigel set his cup down.

The waitress stopped to check whether they were ready to order, then left again.

"How's that?" Lane wrapped his fingers around the cup, absorbing as much heat as possible.

"I see the details, the little things. You see the big picture. You like to think about what's happening, and I need to talk about it." Nigel looked nervously around him.

Lane saw the worry lines across Nigel's forehead. "You think we have a problem?"

"I think I'm not helping the way I should." Nigel hesitated as the waitress returned.

"Ready now?" She smiled.

Lane said. "Bacon and eggs. Eggs over medium. Whole-wheat toast, please."

The waitress turned to Nigel, who said, "Same with scrambled eggs, please."

Lane waited for the waitress to leave. "I think it's just the opposite, actually. We come at the case from different points of view. It means we'll see more angles if we work at it from both viewpoints."

Nigel frowned. "I'm not sure."

"Look." Lane put his coffee cup down. A passing waitress filled it up. Nigel shook his head. "You look at the details, and you like to talk it out. I look at the big picture and like to think it out. When those two different approaches come together, we have a better chance of finding the key to unlocking this one."

"So, you think we have a key?" Nigel asked.

"A lock, at least. I've been reading over some of the files. Byron Thomas had jewellery from another break-in. It was a gold necklace from a burglary ten months before. The necklace did not come from the Bannerman house. It was identified as taken from a house in the southwest. The Bannerman murder was in the northwest. How did Byron Thomas get to the house in the southwest? I checked the map. According to one report, Byron liked to work within three kilometres of an LRT station. He would pick cans and bottles out of the blue boxes in the neighborhoods on the days they had garbage pickup. The house in the southwest is ten kilometres from the nearest LRT station and twelve from the nearest bottle recycler. It doesn't fit his pattern." Lane added sugar and cream to his refreshed coffee.

"How did I miss that?" Nigel asked.

"That's what I mean. What one of us misses, the other sees. I got that one because I was driving to the hospital from work. I remembered how often I see homeless people near bottle depots. There's a bottle depot near my place, and last summer I would see a guy going through my blue box early on the morning of the day of garbage pickup. It made me think, and when I looked back at the investigative reports I found the anomaly." Lane stirred his coffee. "There's nothing else to connect him to the Bannerman murder. No fingerprints. Nothing but the necklace and the blood on his shoe. The blood can be explained by his being in the house. It doesn't prove he's the killer."

Nigel sat back, looking at the entrance to the restaurant. "I have an idea I need to check." He began to stand up.

Lane held up his hand. "Eat first."

After returning to the office, they spent the rest of the afternoon mapping the remainder of the information on the big screen. By the time seven o'clock rolled around, neither one could focus on what was in front of him.

"See you in the morning?" Lane asked.

Nigel nodded.

Twenty minutes later, Lane was driving west along the south side of the Bow River. It was insulated with its winter outfit of ice and snow. Foggy condensation rose over open patches of fast-moving water. Ahead of him was a fog of exhaust from vehicles. Not for the first time, he thanked Arthur for his insistence they get heated seats in this vehicle.

Ten minutes later, he pulled into the parkade at the Children's Hospital, leaving the warmed-up car and beginning the long walk to the hallway and the main foyer. He went upstairs, following the red line on the floor. He walked past the paintings on the wall, past the nursing station, opening the door to Indiana's room. A woman sat in the chair just inside the door. She held her breast up to her infant's mouth.

Lane backed out the door. "Sorry!"

The woman ignored him. The door closed. Lane backed up and his right heel hit the base of the wall. It seemed the organs inside his chest were about to implode. Sweat gathered along his hairline. He looked down the hallway toward the nursing station. *Slow down! Stop panicking!*

"Your phone is beeping."

Lane looked to his left and saw a small boy with a teddy bear stuck under his arm. He wore a pair of jeans, white running shoes, and a red T-shirt. "This is for my little sister." He held the bear out front.

Lane heard his phone beep again. He pulled it out of the inside pocket of his sports jacket, pressing a button on the face. A text message read, "Don't go to hospital. Indy, Christine, and Dan at home."

chapter 6

"You look like..." Nigel hesitated.

"Shit?" Lane watched the traffic in the outside lane.

"Tired. Baby come home?"

Lane nodded. *He doesn't need to know about the way I reacted when I found someone else in Indiana's room, freezing instead of using my head.*

Nigel checked left, easing around a green Ford with two women in the front seat talking with their hands. The car swerved into their lane. Nigel hit the horn and the brakes.

Lane got a glimpse of the wide-open mouth and eyes of the passenger. The driver continued to talk with her hands. The passenger grabbed the wheel. The vehicle straightened out.

"Hazards of sign language," Nigel said.

Lane looked at the clock. "Okay if I take a look around inside while you get the pictures?"

Nigel nodded, gliding past another vehicle. "No worries."

They parked in the LRT station lot, walking across the street to the funeral home. The wind was calm, the sun was out, and the forecast said the temperature was supposed to warm to minus ten. Lane looked at his watch. *I wonder if there's time for a coffee?*

"Don't worry, we'll get a coffee after." Nigel hefted the Nikon with the long lens, looking for an inconspicuous spot where he could snap the mourners walking in.

"You sure you want to stay outside and take pictures?" Lane adjusted his blue tie to ensure the knot was centred.

Nigel cradled the camera in his arms. "I'm sure."

Lane looked at his partner. Nigel's eyes darted left and right. His black toque was pulled down over his ears, riding his eyebrows. Lane saw the freckles on Nigel's cheeks. A cloud of his breath hung in the air. Lane asked, "This case has got to you, hasn't it?"

Nigel locked on his partner's eyes. "Let's just catch the fuckers."

Lane nodded, crossed the street, walked to the entrance of the funeral home, and stepped inside. He knocked the snow off his shoes, unzipped his winter coat, and looked around. To his right was a wall of oak-framed windows and beyond that the chapel with its obligatory stained glass. To his left, the office and a broad staircase leading upstairs. A woman in a navy-blue jacket and calf-length skirt asked, "Can I help you?"

Lane smiled, reaching inside his suit jacket pocket and pulling out his ID. "I'm with the Calgary Police Service."

The woman frowned, then turned her head slightly with disapproving half-closed eyes.

"Melissa and David Randall are aware I'm here. I'd like to sit to one side." Lane eased his left arm out of the sleeve of his winter jacket.

The woman used her left hand to indicate direction, walking into the chapel and turning left. Lane followed her to the far left of the chapel. "Front or rear?" she asked.

"Front, please. I need to see faces." She led him up front. He sat down against the wall. "Thank you."

The woman nodded and left.

Lane folded his coat over the seat next to him and looked at the grey wall beside him. He looked at his grey sportcoat. *I'll blend right in. Just put on the face and disappear.* "The face" was a survival technique Lane had learned as a child. It allowed him to fade into the background, a way of flying below the radar of recognition.

Mourners began to trickle in. David Randall walked in a side door followed by a girl of about fourteen. She wore a black jacket, black pants, and red pumps. Her black hair was cut short.

David said, "Come on, Beth, I just need to check and make sure everything is working."

Beth looked at Lane; then her green eyes moved on to the back of the chapel where people were gathered. David touched a computer screen. It lit his face with blue light.

Lane thought, *He looks like he's lost maybe ten pounds.*

"I already made sure everything is working. Besides, Aunty Peggy is here." Beth's voice was filled with a sarcastic blend of loathing and anxiety.

David looked over his shoulder, staring at his daughter, opening his mouth, closing it. "Can we just get through this without any drama?"

"Why is she here?" Beth turned to her father, looking for something to attack.

When you're fourteen and angry, you have to take it out on someone.

David turned to the projector. A picture of his mother and father appeared on the screen. They were on a beach, smiling, leaning into each other, with Beth tucked under her grandfather's arm. A smaller boy stood next to Elizabeth.

"How come you never stand up to Aunt Peggy?" Beth looked up at the image. "She was mad because we went to Mexico with Poppa and Nanny, remember?"

David shut off the projector. "What good would it do?"

"You're such a wimp!" Beth turned around, her posture stiff with anger, and stomped out the side door.

David's shoulders sagged. He turned to follow.

A seismic wave of braying laughter rolled through the chapel. Lane and David looked toward the main doorway at the back of the chapel. A woman with dyed-red hair, painted-on eyebrows, a six-foot frame, an oversized head, and a white dress threw her head back and performed again. She leaned on a Malacca cane. The posse of women surrounding her added lemming laughter.

Lane watched David's face redden. The man stepped forward, then retreated out the side door.

The voices outside the main doorway grew louder. People trickled in, sitting on benches. Lane looked at his watch and saw there were only five minutes before the service was to start. The woman with the eyebrows stood in the doorway with two other women. They were deep in conversation, a car wreck in the centre of a downtown intersection. Behind them, people gathered, waiting to get inside.

The funeral director opened the side door, walking in front of Lane, then over to the blocked doorway. He smiled and took Aunt Peggy by the arm, guiding her like a bouncing front-end loader down a roadway to the front bench on the family side. Behind her, the other rows of pews filled with people until every seat was taken. Only a handful of seats next to Peggy remained.

Lane saw the suits and glittering jewellery. The carefully trimmed hair of the men and the elaborately coloured, stylishly coiffed cuts of the women. *It's been a while since I've been to one of these. The last time it was Dad's funeral and I had to leave early. I remember the light coming in through the stained glass.* He looked at the paired stained-glass windows behind the podium. They faced north, illuminated by reflected light. He saw David and Melissa set paper atop the lectern in front of the windows. Melissa wore a fitted red jacket, black blouse, and black pants. To their left a pair of brass urns held the cremated remains of their parents.

David lifted his head, beginning to speak even though many people in the chapel were still talking. "Thank you for coming to celebrate the lives of our parents." His throat constricted with emotion, and he stopped. Some people in the pews continued to talk.

Lane looked right to see Aunt Peggy talking with the man and woman behind her. Lane turned back to the front.

Melissa put her left hand on the shoulder of her brother's navy-blue sports jacket. She said, "Our parents did well with their business and thought it was important to give back to the community. They believed in deeds more than words. So we wanted to tell their story in pictures."

A photograph of their much-younger parents was projected on the screen. They were tucked in close to each other, the Chateau Lake Louise in the background. It was summer. The lake was glacial blue.

A series of slides followed. Lane turned to watch the faces of the people in the chapel, systematically moving from row to row, face to face. He heard Melissa say, "Mom's maiden name was McKenzie. We used to spend time in the summer in the Shuswap with our cousins from her side of the family."

Lane spotted a couple of smiles from people who must have been her cousins. Another voice broke in. The smiles morphed into rage. "And we are proud of that name McKenzie!" Lane searched to find the face behind the voice. Aunt Peggy said, "I insisted on keeping my last name when I got married. I think there is reason to be proud of a name." The voice was filled with implied superiority.

There was movement to Lane's right. Beth stood up. Melissa stopped Beth with a smile. Beth sat down.

Lane looked up at a picture of the family sitting around a campfire in lawn chairs. A setting sun painted the lake waters in the background. Something nagged at the edges of understanding. He went back to cataloguing faces and impressions. He spotted a familiar face. Megan Newsome, neighbour to the Randalls, sat next to a man in a tailored black suit. On her other side sat half a dozen women with stylishly cut hair. Lane noted one was at least twenty years younger than the others.

"My grandmother and my grandfather took care of me before I went to school."

Lane turned to look at the new speaker. Beth stood between her father and her aunt. "They took my brother and me for a holiday to Mexico for two weeks this winter. They took us to see Chichen Itza, and they took us to a place where the sea turtles nest. It was magical, and it is a memory I will hold close." An image of Beth, her grandparents, and her little brother appeared on the screen. They stood in the tropical sun with the main pyramid at Chichen Itza behind them. Lane was struck by what had escaped him from the beginning of the memorial. *The Randalls were a functional family*.

David said, "Thank you for coming. Just a reminder about signing the guest book, and please join us for the reception upstairs." Music began to play. Lane recognized Vivaldi's *Four Seasons*. People began to stand and file out. Lane took the side door, making his way to the foyer where people were taking the stairs to the reception. He followed them, stopped, turned, and stood at the railing to observe goings-on down below.

Aunt Peggy, looking remarkably agile for a woman with a cane, made for the elevator, passing out of sight beneath him.

"But I saw you there that night." The woman's voice came from behind him. He turned, looking to find the person behind the words. A crowd of mourners shuffled through the double doors leading to the reception. He looked at the backs of people's heads. Megan Newsome looked to her right. Lane saw she was surrounded by a quartet of carefully coiffed heads in various shades ranging from brunette to blonde.

The elevator door slid open. Aunt Peggy sprinted out, joining the crush.

"Anyone in particular you want me to get a shot of?" Nigel stood next to him, his earlobes and nose red from the cold.

Lane pointed at the clutch of hair approaching the doorway.

Nigel lifted the camera above his head. The flash fired. People turned. The flash fired again to illuminate several faces, including Megan Newsome's.

"Good," Lane said.

Nigel faced his partner. "Your voice has changed."

Furrows appeared on Lane's forehead as he turned to Nigel. "What?"

"Oh." Nigel turned away.

"What?"

"It's just —" Nigel unzipped his jacket.

"Well?"

"You sound different than when you were in the car."

"Oh." *How do I explain I know the killer is in this crowd?*

×

"Uncle, can you hold Indiana? Dan is sleeping, and I want to have a bath." Christine sat on the couch in the family room. Indiana was tucked in the crook of her elbow. His face and thick black hair were visible despite the floral blanket cocoon.

"Glad to." Lane sat down in the easy chair, waiting as she brought the baby over to him. Indiana was warm against his chest. A tiny hand appeared from under the blanket. Lane found himself counting fingers.

"You don't mind?" Christine asked.

"You're kidding, right? I love holding him." He watched as Indiana frowned. The white dressing on his forehead moved up, then down.

"Matt and Uncle Arthur took Alex shopping for clothes." She put her hand on her uncle's shoulder.

Lane looked up at her, raising his eyebrows.

"For Indiana. They went shopping for clothes for him." She hesitated. "Do you love him?"

"What's not to love? He's beautiful."

"My mother called you Pauline. Was it what they called you when you were growing up?" Christine asked.

Lane nodded.

"Is it the reason why you don't like to be called by your first name?"

Lane nodded.

"I'll be quick." Christine turned and went upstairs.

Lane watched Indiana's face. He heard Dan snoring in the bedroom. He heard Christine turn on the water in the bathtub. Then he looked at his reflection in the black of the TV screen. One of the pictures from the Randall funeral rose up to the surface of his memory: an image of Robert Randall holding a newborn Beth. Lane forced himself to relax his jaw to keep from clenching his teeth. Then his memory projected the image of Robert Randall's head, his brains spattered over the wall and ceiling.

Fifteen minutes later, Christine came downstairs wearing sweats, a T-shirt, and a white towel around her head.

"Go lie down. He's sleeping. I'd just like to sit here and hold him."

"Wake me up in half an hour." Christine caressed Indiana's cheek with the back of her forefinger, then went into the bedroom, closing the door.

An hour later, Matt, Arthur, and Alex arrived with a stomping of feet and a swell of cold air flowing down the steps. Sam wagged his tail, whimpering hello.

Arthur looked down the stairs and saw Lane with the baby. Lane put his finger to his lips.

"The baby's asleep," Arthur whispered. Three faces looked down the stairs, smiling.

Within thirty minutes, everyone but Lane and Indiana was tucked away in bed while the Randall case ran a marathon in Lane's mind.

A little after one, Lane heard footsteps in the upstairs hallway. A few minutes later, the toilet flushed. He turned on the TV, watching a movie without any sound.

"Uncle?"

Lane opened his eyes.

"Why didn't you wake me up?" Christine had her new mother I'm-the-protector-of-this-child look in her eyes.

Lane studied a still-sleeping Indiana. "What time is it?"

"Six. I asked you to wake me up after half an hour." Christine picked up the baby. "He's wet."

Lane looked at his shirt, seeing he was wet too.

"Sorry."

chapter 7

"They need us down in Kensington." Nigel's voice on the phone was businesslike.

Lane looked at their kitchen chaos. Bottles waiting to be washed, the countertop needing a wipe, the dishwasher needing to be run, a tea towel on the floor in front of the stove, the microwave timer beeping to tell him the coffee was ready in the Bodum. "How many dead?"

"Two."

"In a house?"

"Nope. On a fire escape behind a bookstore. So dress warm. Fibre is on his way. I'll pick you up in fifteen." Nigel hung up.

Lane had time to shower and put on layers of cotton and fleece underneath his polyester-shell winter jacket. He tied up his winter boots and stepped outside. The sun was bright. It reflected off the snow on the street and the front lawn. A white cloud from a passing car's exhaust told him the same thing as his nostrils when he inhaled the January air: it was at least minus twenty. He walked down the front steps, climbing in the passenger side of the Chev. "Thanks for warming it up." Lane closed the door, stuffing his black leather gloves on the dash and reaching for his seat belt.

"No worries." Nigel pulled away. The Chev's tires crunched over the compacted snow.

"What have we got?" Lane unzipped his jacket.

"Two bodies, a male and a female. They're both sitting on an outside stairway in a back alley." Nigel looked sideways at Lane. "That's a first."

"What?" Lane tried to peer through the fog of exhaust as the cars in front of them accelerated when the light turned green.

"You haven't shaved."

Lane reached up, rubbing the shadow on his cheek. "Busy night. Indiana and I stayed up late working on the case."

Nigel steered the car down Sarcee Trail. They looked over the valley where the exhaust from chimneys puffed into the arctic air. Lane looked east at the downtown where white smoke rose above the cigarette-shaped high-rises. The smoke flattened out at about five hundred metres.

Nigel said, "It'll be nice when the warmer air decides to come down to ground level." He steered the Chev along Crowchild Trail on their way into Kensington. Ten minutes later, he pulled into an alley running parallel to Memorial Drive with houses on the south and businesses on the north. They stopped behind a white-stuccoed two-storey building with black-framed windows and a metal stairway. It switch-backed to a second-storey door. Two forms huddled facing each other where the switchback turned east to west within a few feet of the white cinderbrick wall of the Plaza Theatre.

Down below, Fibre's Forensic Crime Scene Unit was parked beside a red Volvo. Nigel left the Chev running as they got out, ducking under the yellow crime scene tape and zipping their jackets to shield against the cold. Nigel pointed at the Volvo's licence plate. "Kind of ironic."

Lane spotted the LVS4EVR Alberta plate, looked more closely at the scene. "Another tableau."

Nigel turned to him. "You really think so?"

Lane nodded. "It's staged. The bodies were carried up to where the stairway turns back on itself. Look at the set of tracks leading up to the stairway. The licence plate on the car is another convenient coincidence. It's got the earmarks of a staged scene."

"Lives forever." Nigel shook his head. "This is one sick bastard."

Lane watched Dr. Weaver, wearing his white bunny suit, step onto the bottom rung of the staircase. The metal steps thrummed on contact at this temperature. *He looks like the Michelin man. He must be wearing a skidoo suit under there.* Fibre stepped onto the second rung, taking photographs at each step. He made his way up to the first body dressed in a black wool overcoat. The body leaned up against the railing where it sat with its hands hanging between its knees. He called down to his assistant sitting in the cab of the van. "Male. Bullet wound to the forehead." He stepped around the first body and onto the landing, looking down. He reached into the pocket of his bunny suit, set down a ruler, and snapped another photograph. He turned to the second body, which leaned against the wall of the building, facing the first. This one was dressed in a grey evening gown. "Female. No apparent entry or exit wound."

"Try the mouth," Lane said.

Fibre looked down at Lane, then turned back to the body. He put his left hand on the deceased's jaw. "Frozen. It looks like there is some gunpowder residue on the lips. It will have to wait for autopsy."

Lane felt dread at the pit of his stomach. "Any ID on the bodies?"

Fibre stared at the detective when he heard the tone of Lane's voice. "I haven't checked the pockets. No purse at the scene."

"May I come up?" Lane asked.

Fibre looked down at the metal steps, then glanced to the right. "There is a patch of ice up here with a layer of snow and a footprint. Be careful of that."

Lane reached for the railing. He watched where he put his feet on the sawtooth tread of the stairway. The metal sang out each time the sole of his boot made contact. He eased past the body of the man, looking into the frozen face of Megan Newsome.

"You know who it is, then?" Fibre asked.

"I do." Lane eased down the steps, looking down between his feet, calculating the placement of each backward step.

Fibre did the same. "Name?"

"Megan Newsome. The male will probably be her husband."

Fibre walked over to the cab of the van. Lane and Nigel couldn't hear what he said to his colleague over the rattle of the diesel engine.

The cab door of the van opened. Fibre approached the detectives. "The store owner's inside waiting for you. Use the front door."

"How are the kids, Colin?" Lane worked at keeping his voice calm. *The woman's voice at the funeral. 'But I saw you there that night.' It was Megan Newsome.*

Fibre smiled. "Good. How is the baby?"

Lane looked at the doctor. "How did you know?"

Fibre tapped his nose with a forefinger. "I have my sources." He walked to the back of the van, opened the door, and pulled out a toolbox.

Nigel and Lane walked east along the alley, turning left and then left again at the lights. They walked past restaurants and the Plaza Theatre before entering via the front door of Pages Books. They stepped into the warmth. The hardwood floors creaked as Lane took in the rows of books and the stairway to the second floor.

Two women sat behind the counter. One had dark-brown hair and wore a black-and-red shawl around her shoulders. The other had shoulder-length grey hair and sat behind a computer screen. They eyed the detectives with a combination of annoyance, interest, and distrust.

"Which one of you discovered the bodies?" Lane took off his gloves and toque.

The grey-haired woman looked at the other woman, who said, "I did. Wouldn't it be easier if we started with names?"

"I'm Detective Lane, and this is Detective Li." Lane waited.

The brown-haired woman took a long breath. "Simone."

"Sarah." The grey-haired woman sitting behind the computer screen stood up.

Lane looked at the women, thought for a moment, looked out the back window, then turned to look across Kensington Road. "Anybody want a Rolo?"

"Took the words out of my mouth." Simone went to the back of the store, grabbed two coats, and handed one to Sarah.

"Any sign of a break-in?" Nigel asked.

"None." Sarah pulled on her coat, stepping out from behind the counter. She wore tan leather boots reaching her knees. Her black slacks and top looked stylish and practical.

Simone pulled a pack of cigarettes out of the pocket of her red coat. She lit up as she opened the door, waiting outside for the detectives to follow. Sarah locked the door.

They picked their way through the snow piled alongside the road by a passing snowplow, waiting for a gap in traffic, crossing the road, and climbing the stairs to Higher Ground. Simone carefully stubbed out her cigarette on the stone railing. Inside they found a fire burning in the centre of the room, light streaming through the glass ceiling to the left, various conversations at the tables, and a line-up for coffee. Nigel took the orders, then looked at Lane. "I'll get this. You see if you can find a table."

They found a pair of leather chairs near the back under the glass roof. Lane borrowed two chairs from other tables. He found himself sitting across from Sarah and Simone.

Sarah said, "I got to the store first. Didn't notice anything wrong."

Simone hung her winter coat over the back of her chair. Lane got the distinct impression Simone had a poor opinion of police officers. "I parked at the back of the store and saw the couple on the stairway. We get all sorts of neighbourhood regulars around here, but they didn't look familiar. I got out of the car, called out to them. When they didn't answer, I went closer and saw the man's eyes were open. Then I saw the third eye."

"She came in the back door and called 911." Sarah crossed one leg over the other.

Lane sat back in his chair. "Do either of you recognize the victims?"

They looked at each other and turned back to face him, shaking their heads.

Nigel arrived with a Rolo for Simone and tea for Sarah.

"Thank you," the women said.

He returned with a Rolo for Lane and a cappuccino for himself, then sat down next to his partner. For a few minutes they all sipped their drinks, wrapping their fingers around the warmth radiating from the ceramic mugs.

Lane focused on Simone. "What does your licence plate mean, exactly?"

"The King lives forever." Simone took a sip of coffee.

"She's an Elvis fan." Sarah put her tea down on the pizza-pan–sized coffee table.

Nigel asked, "Any customers stick out in your memories this last little while?"

"You think this has something to do with my licence plate?" Simone looked at Lane with disbelief.

Lane shrugged. "At this point, we're looking at any and all variables."

"Variables?" Simone made no attempt to mask the sarcasm.

Lane said, "Someone put the bodies on your steps. They were placed facing each other."

Simone pointed a finger at Lane. "They weren't killed at my shop."

Be careful. She's quick. She could still be a suspect, Lane thought. "I'm just saying we're looking at all possibilities so we can track the killers and not get sidetracked looking at the wrong people."

Sarah picked up her tea, watching both detectives over the rim of her mug. "The fact is neither one of us committed the murders. I'm trying to think of any reason why the bodies were placed where they were and coming up with nothing so far."

Simone took a sip of Rolo. "For the last half hour or so we've been trying to figure out why the bodies would be left at the back of the store. It's obvious to us the bodies were intentionally placed facing each other. There's no blood on the snow, so they were killed elsewhere. But why pick Pages?"

Sarah leaned in closer to Lane. "You're that Detective Lane, the one who took down Smoke."

"How'd you know about that?" Nigel asked.

We're along for the ride now. Probably best to just go with it, Nigel.

"There's this retired cop who likes to read crime novels and tell Sarah how the writers got it all wrong. And he talks about what's going on behind the stories in the newspapers." Simone stopped with her cup halfway to her lips. "You think this case is connected to the Randall murders, don't you?"

Nigel looked at Lane, who asked, "Who's your source?"

Sarah said, "People come to buy books, look at books, and some of them like to talk. You'd be surprised how much they tell us."

Simone stared out of the window, then turned to Sarah.

"Do you remember that woman who asked about Homolka, Olson, Pickton, and Colonel Williams?"

Sarah looked at her boss. "You mean the Lulu Lemon bitch?"

Simone smiled, nodding.

Lane concentrated, filtering out the chatter from nearby conversations.

Sarah said, "She came in looking for books on Canadian serial killers. She was pretty upset when we didn't have them on the shelves."

"Did you get a name?" Lane asked.

Sarah shook her head. "She didn't leave a name."

"Just bad air," Simone said.

Lane looked at the women, raising his eyebrows.

Sarah frowned. "Most of the quirky people we get who won't leave their names are tinfoil-on-your-head-paranoid kinda people. They're regulars. She was a make-the-hair-on-the-back-of-your-neck-stand-up kinda person."

"Can you describe her at all?" Lane asked.

Simone pointed at Sarah. "About Sarah's height and weight, and she wore tight yoga pants, running shoes, and a jacket."

Lane waited.

"There was one thing that was odd." Sarah looked up through the glass roof at the blue sky. "There was hair stuck to her pant legs. Lots of hair. You know, like the stuff you get on your clothes when you go to a hair salon."

×

"Are all of the pictures downloaded?" Lane stepped into their office with a coffee in each hand. He set one down on Nigel's desk, holding on to the other while waiting to see the pictures from the funeral.

Nigel reached for his coffee. "Almost. Which ones were you wanting to look at?"

"I'll know when I see them. Let me sit, please."

Nigel got up so Lane could sit in front of the computer. He began to work his way through the pictures until he got to the photo of the group of women entering the doorway to the reception. Megan Newsome's face was caught by the camera's flash, as were the faces of three other women. Only one had her back turned to the camera. Lane pointed at the back of the woman's head. "Have you got a shot of her from the front?"

"Just this." Nigel took the mouse, clicking on a photo taken in front of the building. The woman walked out front of the funeral home. She wore a silver fur coat with a hood covering all but her nose. She held her left hand up to keep the camera side of the hood against her face.

"She knew you were there." Lane sat back in the chair.

"Apparently."

"We need to see the Randall family again." Lane sat up straight.

"When?" Nigel backed away from the computer.

"Now. Can you run copies of both pictures?"

Nigel nodded. "It'll take a couple of minutes."

Nigel parked half a block away from the Randall home. He and Lane got out of the car, zipping up their winter jackets. The northwest wind froze the nose and ears first, then attacked whatever exposed flesh remained even as the sun shone low in a clear blue sky. Lane looked at the cars and SUVs parked in the driveway leading to the grey two-storey. Then he looked across the street at the newly empty Newsome house. There was a fresh skiff of snow filling in the tracks on the driveway. An evergreen tree hid the front windows. White smoke rose from the chimney to warm the house while the bodies of husband and wife chilled in the morgue.

"Lane?" Nigel waited at the bottom of the stairs leading to the Randalls' front door.

Lane shook his head and followed his partner up the stairs. Nigel knocked. They stood waiting for thirty seconds before David's daughter Beth opened the door. She eyed the detectives, opened the door, then closed it quickly behind them. "Thank you." Lane tucked an envelope of photographs under his armpit as he took off his gloves and toque.

Beth said, "My dad and Aunt Melissa are upstairs packing."

Lane unzipped his jacket and bent to untie his laces. He stepped out of his boots and stood up. He saw Nigel staring at the empty front room where the air shone with disinfectant.

"We had the house cleaned. You're the first one to take his boots off. The floors were a mess from the boots and . . ." She held out her hand. "Can I take your jackets?"

Nigel stepped out of his shoes while Lane took off his winter jacket and handed it to Beth. She continued. "We're just looking through my grandparents' stuff before donating everything else. There's a family in need at the women's shelter. We got rid of whatever was in the living room." She took Nigel's jacket, folding their coats over the back of a kitchen chair. They followed her upstairs to a hallway leading to four bedrooms. "Dad's in there." She pointed at the master suite.

Lane poked his head inside a bedroom larger than his family room. He could see the door to the master bath off to the left. There was a Jacuzzi tub at the bottom of a wall made of opaque glass bricks. He saw the back of a tall woman picking through a jewellery box and recognized Aunt Peggy, who was dressed in a pair of stretchy jeans and a black blouse. Lane saw her face reflected in the glass of the mirror atop a dresser made of rosewood. She was intently inspecting one piece at a time. He saw her stuff a gold necklace in a nearby purse the size of a Third World economy. *What happened to her cane?*

Lane stepped inside the room, hearing a sound to his right. His feet silently crossed the carpet until he stood outside of a walk-in closet. Lane saw the wall safe over David Randall's shoulder. David had his back to Lane as he reached up, pulling a box down from the shelf. Lane said, "Anything in the safe?"

David turned. "Just the will." Sweat rolled down the side of his face. He looked past the detective, frowning. "Peg, please leave Mom's jewellery alone."

Peg turned, picking up her purse and tucking it under her arm. "She was my sister!" She insinuated outrage in every syllable.

"I told you the jewellery would be distributed to Melissa and Beth first. Then you will have your turn." David eased past Lane. "Sorry."

Should I tell him about what she's got in the purse?

David looked at her purse, waiting.

Peg asked, "What?"

David lifted his eyebrows.

Peg reached into her bag. She pulled out a broach, gold necklace, three rings, a string of pearls, and an antique Love Story dinner plate. She set each piece on the bed.

David said, "Thanks for all of your help. You can go home now."

Peg glared at him. "I am grieving."

David crossed his arms.

"My sister died. I need to grieve." Peg began to wail, wiping at her eyes.

Lane looked for evidence of a wet shine on Peg's fingers. There was none.

Melissa appeared in the doorway. She looked at the haul on the bed, then at her brother. Lane saw David's reflection in the mirror. *He's exhausted and finally had enough of Aunt Peg.*

"Please leave, Peg." Melissa began to weep. Her tears darkened the front of her white blouse.

"You never liked me. I changed your diapers when you were little!" Peg stepped through the door. A pair of lacey black underwear hung from her back pocket.

"What's that?" David pointed.

Melissa caught a glimpse of the dangling undies before Peg disappeared from view. "Mom's underwear."

They looked at each other. David shook his head. "She had the same parents as Mom."

"And apparently the same taste in underwear." Melissa leaned her head back and howled. At first Lane thought she was crying. Then he heard David's laughter. Sister and brother pointed at each other. Melissa gasped, "She stole Mom's underwear!"

"Remember how Mom would just shake her head at the things Peg would do?" David pointed at a picture on the nightstand. Their mother stood between her grandchildren. She wasn't much taller than Beth. "Remember how she would say, 'Oh, Peg.'?"

The pair began to laugh louder. The uncontrolled, long-bottled-up laughter was some weird combination of release and incredulity. Their spouses arrived in the room, followed by Nigel and Beth. She looked at Lane with confusion.

"Peg stole Mom's underwear!" Melissa managed to say.

The laughter bounced against the frosted glass. It ricocheted off the ceiling and walls.

A few minutes later Lane had the photos set out on the bed. Nigel was entering the names of people identified in the pictures.

"Anyone know who this is?" Lane pointed first at the woman in the hooded fur coat, then at the back of her head in another photo.

Melissa shook her head. David frowned. Beth said, "Looks like one of the hairdressers where Nanny got her hair done."

"Know her name?" Nigel asked.

"Sure. Cori. She works at a place just off of Macleod Trail. Platinum or something like that. Nanny took me there last month for a trim."

Melissa made eye contact with Lane. "You think she's the one who killed our parents, don't you?"

The question sounded rhetorical to Lane's ears so he didn't answer. "What about the other people in this photograph?" He pointed at the clutch of women walking into the reception area.

Melissa reached out and touched Lane's forearm. "I don't sleep much. My mind won't shut down. I keep going over conversations I had with my mom. At night I put on my warmest clothes and go out for a walk. I remember Mom telling me about a group of women she knew, and how they were worried because there were five of them left when there used to be nine. They called themselves the Nine Bottles, because they got together one night and drank nine bottles of wine. They asked Mom to join, but she told me she didn't want to be part of some small-minded clique. Mom hated that kind of shit. She and Dad joined the Rotary Club only after they saw what kind of work the organization did. Anyway, Mom's hairdresser moved into the shop where the Nine Bottles got their hair done. She talked about how she was glad she didn't have to have her hair done by the same person who did the hair of the Nine Bottles. She and Donna used to have a lot of talks about it."

Lane thought, *Roll with it. She may be on to something. Sarah at Pages described the hair on that woman's pants.* "Like what?"

"You should really talk with Donna. I just remember general things she said." Melissa looked at Beth.

"Nanny thought they were losers. The Nine Bottles had to have a girls' night out every week. They went to the same places for clothes. They went on holidays together. They were always talking behind their hands with one another. When Nanny took me to get my hair trimmed, she and Donna started to laugh at something Donna said. She wouldn't tell me what it was about, but I heard anyways. Donna said, "They should have their own reality show. Real Housewives of Mount Royal.'" Beth looked at the pictures on the bed. "That's Donna."

Lane studied the image of a woman with black shoulder-length hair wiping tears from her eyes. She stood apart from the clutch of women gathered around Cori. "Donna's last name?"

"Liu," Melissa said.

Nigel said, "Megan Newsome and her husband were murdered last night."

Lane put his hand on his partner's shoulder.

Melissa blanched. Beth looked to her father. David said, "Fuck."

×

"Go ahead, say it." Nigel drove along Elbow Drive. They were climbing out of the river valley. The car slipped, then gripped as tires searched for traction. The hard-packed snow had turned to ice after the steady passage of vehicles.

Lane shook his head. *What the hell were you thinking?*

"You think I shouldn't have mentioned the Newsomes." Nigel put his foot down on the accelerator. One tire whirred, whining as it spun on the ice. He backed off the pedal.

"We need to talk with next of kin first." Lane took a long, slow breath. *Getting angry with him won't help the situation.*

"I wanted to know if they were involved in the Newsome killing. That's all." Nigel reached the crest of the hill. The Chev began to accelerate.

"Well?"

"My gut tells me they weren't."

"What about Aunt Peg?"

"Her I'm not so sure about." The light ahead turned red. Nigel took his foot off the accelerator. He coasted up to the lights, looking in his rear-view mirror.

"What?"

"Big pickup behind me. You know, knobby tires, jacked-up frame, winch, dark paint. All I can see is the grille."

With the roar of a diesel engine, the truck moved within centimetres of the Chev's rear bumper. The truck driver put his foot on the brakes, pressing the accelerator. The wind carried a cloud of coal-black soot forward. Lane undid his seat belt and, as the cloud diffused, opened his door, walked around the front of the Chev, and pulled out his ID, holding it above his head. He slipped on a patch of ice, regained his balance, stepped up to the side of the truck, and knocked on the middle of the door. He stepped right of the door, noticing Nigel had the blue-and-red flashing lights on. Lane felt the nip of the January air on his fingers and ears. He put his free hand on his Glock.

The door cracked open. The face of a forty-year-old man glared down at Lane. The detective held up his ID so the driver could get a closer look. "Bring your licence, registration, and insurance when you step down, please." Lane looked over his shoulder to see how traffic was doing behind them. A man in a sub-compact with snow on the roof smiled at Lane. He looked left as the pickup driver climbed down from the cab. He was a full head shorter than the detective, wearing a backwards-facing ball cap and a red-and-black prairie dinner jacket. Lane gestured the man should follow him to the sidewalk.

"Look, I'm sorry, I didn't know you were a cop." The man handed his paperwork over, tucking his hands under his armpits. He was round in the face and belly.

Nigel appeared on the passenger side of the Chev. Lane shook his head, leaning it to the left. Nigel headed back into the Chev.

Lane read the name on the driver's licence. "Bill?"

The man nodded, stepping up onto the curb. Then he looked back at the detective. They were eye to eye. Lane looked down at his toes where they bumped up against the curb, but he remained at pavement level.

Bill looked down at his feet, then back at Lane, who saw an expression of confusion.

Surprise, Lane thought. "I've got murders to solve."

Bill pointed at his chest with his right forefinger. "I..."

Lane shook his head and held out Bill's ID, waiting for the man to grab it. "I've got no time for this shit."

Bill nodded. "Thanks for that." He looked down at his feet.

Lane shrugged, turned, and got back in the Chev. The light turned green. Nigel eased into the intersection. Lane turned, watching Bill following at a very safe distance.

"You sure you still want to go to Platinum? It's Sunday. They'll be closed."

Lane looked ahead as the road took a dogleg to the right. "I have an idea and I want to get the lay of the land."

chapter 8

Child Abductors to Appear in Court

Efram Milton, his wife Alison Milton, and Lyle Pratt appear in court in Calgary tomorrow to answer charges of attempted child abduction.

The three were arrested last Wednesday night at the Foothills Medical Centre. They allegedly attempted to abduct a newborn boy with the intent of transporting him to an undisclosed location in Utah. All three are members of Paradise, a polygamist community approximately 150 kilometres south of the city.

Crown Prosecutor Lilian Choi said, "These three plotted to kidnap an infant and hide him from his mother. The accused pose a considerable flight risk. I will ask that they be remanded in custody until a trial date can be set."

A fourteen-year-old female accompanying the trio was released into the custody of her uncle.

Lori stood up from behind her computer screen. She held up the newspaper, pointing at an article. Lane could see she wore a blue knit sweater, a white scarf, and blue wool slacks. "You still have a way to go before you're back in my good books."

Lane set down the cardboard tray of drinks he'd brought with him. He lifted a cup of tea out of the tray, setting it next to Lori's keyboard.

"Really?" Lori folded the paper into quarters, setting it down next to the tray. She pointed at the headline. "Just what gives them the right to come after Indiana?" Lori's complexion moved into the red zone.

Lane nodded. He took off his winter jacket, put it over his arm, and lifted the tray with two coffees. The detective cocked his head to the right. Lori followed him into his office. He hung his jacket over the back of his chair, set a coffee down on Nigel's desk, then pulled out the last cup, took a sip, and closed the door. "Sarah, my sister's daughter, said they were planning to take Indiana to some compound near St. George, Utah."

"In the desert north of Vegas?" Lori pulled the tea bag from her cup, swinging it with a wet *thunk* into the garbage can.

Lane nodded. "Apparently there are polygamist communities near there. Indiana is home now."

"And you think I've forgiven you for keeping this to yourself?" Lori set her tea down so she could cross her arms.

Lane opened his mouth, then closed it again.

"Your entire family must still be on edge after what happened to Matt."

Lane shrugged. "They are."

Lori gave him a look, the Lori look that said *Don't bullshit me.*

"I need your help. I want you to go and get your hair done."

Lori laughed. "You need my help? You think you can

change the subject by telling me to get my hair done? That's pretty pathetic."

"Four of the women killed have the same hairdresser."

"Four? I thought it was two."

"Four."

Lori laughed again. "You want me to get my hair done so I can be number five?"

"I just want to send you to the salon. You get your hair done and tell me what you see while you're there." Lane took a sip of coffee. "Nigel and I will be right next door."

"What's next door?"

"A bicycle shop." Lane felt his face heat up.

"You don't think hanging around in a bicycle shop in the middle of January will look a bit suspicious?" She shook her head and picked up her tea, watching Lane.

"You're enjoying this, aren't you?"

"You betcha. Next time you let me know what's goin' on. That's how I stay so well connected. And that's how I keep your ass out of the flames. So, you think if I get out of the office to get my hair done, all will be forgiven? This is a funny way of saying you're sorry."

"The woman's name is Donna Liu, and she works at Platinum."

"Is she the killer?" Lori looked left at Lane's extra-wide computer screen.

Lane shook his head. "I don't think so. It's Cori I want you to watch."

Lori nodded. "Will I use my real name?"

"No. Use a fake name. I'll get you a cell phone with a new number you will use to contact Donna. That way you won't be traceable. If you see any sign of trouble, I want you out of there." Lane set his coffee down. "You can say no for any number of reasons, including the fact this is outside your job description and outside of normal procedure."

"Then why are you asking me?"

Lane smiled. "Because I trust your judgement, and you know people."

"I do know people." She pointed a finger at Lane. "You got a phone number?"

Lane handed her a compact pink phone. She took it gingerly. "Where'd you get this?"

Lane raised his eyebrows.

Lori dropped her chin, lifted her eyebrows, and rolled her eyes.

"Okay. I've got some phones left over from when Matt and Jessica were kidnapped. That's one of them."

"Was that so hard? Now, what was Platinum's number again?"

Lane read out the number, and Lori dialed. She gave him the thumbs up when the phone began to ring. "Hello, I'd like to make an appointment for a cut and trim with Donna." She raised her eyebrows. "A cancellation? This afternoon?" Lori looked at Lane, who nodded. "I'll take it. Two o'clock? My name? Ute. That's right. New client. See you this afternoon." Lori looked at the phone, pressing the end button. "We're on."

Lane smiled. "Ute?"

Lori rolled her eyes. "Ute was my grandmother's name."

×

Lane and Nigel sat in a Vietnamese restaurant within a snowball's throw of Macleod Trail. Lane looked at the traffic easing along the six-lane roadway leading either to the centre of town or south toward the US border. Hoods and windshields glinted in the sunlight. Exhaust swirled from tail pipes. On either side of the road, pedestrians wore mitts, toques, and winter jackets to hold out the cold. Inside the restaurant, a man at a nearby table slurped spicy noodle soup. Nigel frowned at the noise. "I still can't believe you did this."

Lane reached for his water. The waitress, who looked to be seventeen, had rouge on her cheeks, blue makeup around her brown eyes, a ponytail, and graceful fingers. "Ready to order?" She adjusted her white blouse to reveal the top of a blue camisole.

"What's your best soup?" Nigel asked.

"You like spicy?" There was a husky edge to her voice.

Nigel nodded.

"The satay beef will warm you up on a day like this." She looked at Lane.

Nigel said, "I'll go with that."

"Me too. And thank you." Lane handed her his menu and smiled.

The waitress smiled back, taking both menus and walking to the counter outside the kitchen. A middle-aged man with a round face and body to match watched from behind the counter, smiling at Lane.

"Male or female?" Nigel asked.

Lane looked back at Nigel. "Does it make a difference?"

"Just wondering. She looks like a she, but her hands and her voice lead me to believe otherwise." Nigel reached for his water.

Lane shrugged. "She is who she is, and she is very nice to us."

"What's that supposed to mean?"

Lane shook his head. "You hit a nerve."

✕

Lori thumbed through a magazine on hairstyles. Perfect faces, perfect teeth, perfect makeup appeared on every air-brushed page. She thought, *I hope Donna is good at what she does. If she fucks up my hair, Lane is going to get an earful.*

"Ute?" a voice called.

Lori continued to look at the styles and faces in the magazine.

"Ute?"

That's me! Lori stood up, grabbing her purse and looking at a woman with shoulder-length black hair wearing a yellow shirt reaching mid thigh. Donna wore black tights under the shirt and a pair of tan high-heeled boots reaching her knees.

"Come on over. I'm Donna." She led the way to a chair in the middle of three, facing a counter and a mirror the size of a coffee table.

Lori sat down, tucking the heels of her boots over the bar at the bottom of the chair. Donna took out a black cape to cover Lori, attaching it snugly around her neck. Lori watched in the mirror as Donna touched her hair.

Donna said, "What are you looking for?"

A killer. "A trim, and touch up the grey. And ... make me look twenty years younger."

"If I knew how to do that, I would have a big office, a chef, and a personal trainer for hot yoga."

Lori laughed, then saw a white cell phone dancing on the counter.

Donna hesitated.

"Go ahead."

Donna reached for the phone. "My mom is on her way to China. I asked my brother to call when they get there." She pressed a button on the phone. "You made it okay?" Donna listened.

Lori tried not to be obvious while listening in.

"So, Mom's feeling okay? She's hungry? That's a good sign. Thanks for calling." Donna put the phone back on the counter.

"You're close to your mom?"

"Yes. She's back in China for the first time since we left over thirty years ago. It's a big deal for her."

"You're lucky to be close to your mom."

"Very." Donna lifted a strand of Lori's hair, making eye contact in the mirror. "Short? Long?"

"I like it longer." *If this turns out to be a mistake, Lane will owe me 'til the day he retires!*

"How about the colour? You want it a shade darker or lighter?" Donna studied her client's reaction.

Lori saw the intensity in those eyes, recognizing the intelligence behind them. "What do you think?"

Donna looked at Lori in the mirror. "I'd go just a shade darker."

"Okay."

A woman of approximately forty-five in yoga pants and a tight-fitting top pushed open the swinging half doors leading to a smallish lunchroom with a fridge, sink, and hand-me-down chrome kitchen table. Lori spotted the blonde woman with the short hair and felt the tension in Donna's fingers.

The woman said, "Here, I've got these for you. Give them a try." She walked over to a woman with tin foil in her hair, handing her a black wrist strap. The customer sat on a black faux-leather couch, reading a magazine.

"Who's that?" Lori used a volume and a tone only Donna would be able to hear.

"Cori. A stylist. She sells magnetic bracelets and anklets on the side."

Lori heard the dismissal in Donna's tone. "What's your mom like?"

"Cool."

"You're lucky. Mine was a manipulative, psychotic, self-centred narcissist." Lori watched Donna looking across the salon where Cori watched herself in the mirror as she styled the client's hair.

Donna began adding layers of silver paper to Lori's hair. Donna said, "There's a lot of that going around."

That began a fifteen-minute discussion of mothers. They laughed at a few of Lori's funny stories and more of Donna's.

Donna finished up with the colour. The chemical stink of it caught at the back of Lori's throat. Donna reached for a timer and set it. "You want coffee or tea while we wait for the colour?"

"Tea, please." Lori sat down on the black couch where she had a good view of Cori's chair.

"How do you take it?" Donna asked.

"Just tea, please." Lori picked up a magazine, sitting back, pretending to flip through it while observing Cori.

A boy of fifteen or sixteen with black hair, tight jeans, and a blue smock set three folded towels down on the countertop. Cori looked at the towels, reaching over and patting him on the cheek. "Thank you, Robert. You're a doll."

Robert's face turned red. He retreated to a back room.

Cori turned to her client. "You should try that sometime. Young bucks like Robert have endurance." She smiled, beginning to take the silver paper out of her client's hair.

Robert's younger than my son! Lori thought.

Cori's client was a woman between fifty-five and sixty with blonde hair, weighing maybe one hundred thirty pounds. She asked, "What does Andrew have to say about that?"

Cori stopped, smiling at the woman in the mirror. "We have an agreement. I go along with his excursions, and he allows me my diversions."

Donna's timer began to ding. She hustled over, took the silver paper from Lori's hair, then guided her to the sink. Lori sat back. Donna used warm water to wash her hair. Donna's fingers worked their way around Lori's scalp. She began to relax as the scalp massage did its magic. When Donna finished, Lori opened her eyes. "Would you teach my husband how to do that? He thinks that foreplay is something hockey players do at the other end of the rink."

Donna laughed while wrapping Lori's hair in a towel. "Let's get you trimmed. And after I get you looking your best, maybe you'll get some."

Lori saw Cori was moving to the front of the salon. "Sounds like she's looking to get some from Robert. That kid is younger than my son."

"And two years older than my eldest boy. I brought my son here once. Never again." Donna sat Lori down in the chair, removing the towel. She began to trim Lori's hair. "That chick is always after something."

"On the prowl?" Lori watched as Donna's scissors snipped here and there.

"Let's just say I wouldn't want her around my boys. There's something really twisted about her." Donna looked at Lori in the mirror. "Her husband is a professor at the university. She manages to mention he's a PhD in almost every conversation, that he went to Queen's, was a student in her dance class, and he's almost ten years younger than she is."

"How old is she?" Lori watched Cori as she talked with Robert at the front of the store.

"Mid-forties. Travels to all of the hot spots. Has a loyal troop of customers who like to hear about her exploits. Most of them are women whose husbands have done well." Donna reached for the hairdryer.

Lori watched as Cori walked back through the salon, making her way to the washroom.

Donna finished with the dryer and brush, removing the black cape. "Happy?"

Lori looked at the way Donna had framed her face. *John had better notice the new style if he knows what's good for him.* She nodded. "I like it."

Donna smiled, handing Lori a card. "I'm opening my own shop in about six weeks. Call me if you want to set up another appointment."

Lori took the card, stashing it in her purse. She stood up. "Moving on?"

"Something like that." Donna looked at Lori, dropping her volume. "Four months here convinced me to have a shop built in my house. It's more than halfway done."

Go for it. Lori nodded in Cori's direction. "Can't stomach that one going after boys the same age as your son?" She reached into her purse for her wallet.

"Pretty much."

×

Nigel drove them north along Macleod Trail. Traffic was gathering itself, building up to rush-hour intensity. Lori sat in the back seat of the Chev. "So, I would say Cori is a suspect and Donna is not. She senses something is wrong in the salon, sees Cori as the source of it, and is getting out of there." She leaned over to check herself in Nigel's rear-view mirror. "John better notice the new hair or he'll be sleeping on the floor with the dog."

Lane asked, "You're happy with it?" *If Donna made a mess of Lori's hair, I'll never hear the end of it.*

"She's very good. I've been looking for a new hairdresser, and I think I've found her." Lori looked up at the driver of the pickup next to them. "You know what they say about big twucks?"

"What do they say?" Nigel took his foot off the brake as the light turned green.

"Teeny tiny tallywackers. Speaking of tallywackers, Cori appears to prefer hers young — early teens, in fact. I would call her a predator. She did say something rather unusual as well. Let me see if I can recall the exact words." Lori looked left at Chinook Mall as they passed it. "Sure you guys don't want to take me shopping too? I'll buy the coffee."

Lane looked at Nigel, who raised his eyebrows.

"I remember now. Cori said, 'I go along on his excursions and he allows me my diversions.' It was the way she said it that kind of stuck with me. Like she had some big secret and was telling only a bit of the story." She tapped Nigel on the shoulder. "Home, Mr. Li."

An hour later, Lane and Nigel sat looking at the wide screen on Lane's desk.

Nigel said, "I thought I was on to a pair of suspects after checking the passenger lists. They were on two of the flights around the time of the murders in Toronto and New York. The problem is the IDs are bogus."

"Do you have the names?"

"Karly A. Williams and Clayton Olson."

Lane frowned. *What is it about that name?*

Nigel looked at Lane. "I've been thinking about it for the last couple of hours. Do you see it?"

"The Olson is obvious. What about hers?"

"Karly A. as in Karla Homolka and Williams as in Colonel Russell Williams."

"Shit." Lane entered the names on his diagram.

"Exactly." Nigel rubbed his forehead. "What's our next move?"

✕

Lane looked out the window of the LRT car. It rocked from side to side. The wheels hummed as they rolled above the Bow River. The ice on the river wore a fresh coat of snow, softening the rough edges of ice packed up along either side of the river. It had been left there after an early January chinook bathed the city in warm winds and the resultant melt. An overnight drop to minus twenty-five left the middle of the river open in a few places where steam rose into the night. He studied the houses and apartments on the right. In front of one building, a barge of a sedan wore a knitted car cover topped with a red pompom. He smiled.

His phone rang, and he reached for it.

"Where are you?" Matt's voice carried an air of authority.

"On the LRT."

"Where?"

Lane looked out the window at the lights of the Alberta College of Art and Design, a brick building next to an approaching train platform. "ACAD."

"I'll pick you up at Brentwood."

Lane heard and felt the train began to slow. "Which side?"

"The Co-Op side. I'm on my way." Matt ended the conversation and was waiting in the BMW as Lane came down the stairs after crossing the pedestrian bridge over Crowchild Trail. The January wind stung his face as he opened the passenger door and climbed in. He closed the door, feeling the warmth of the heated seat.

"We need another car." Matt pointed over his shoulder at the empty car seat in the back. "I've been driving all over the place. Christine decided she wanted to get out of the house. And Arthur wants to buy some stuff for the baby. Naturally, everyone wanted to come along."

"Where's Alex?" Lane did up his seat belt while they waited at a stoplight.

Matt blushed. "At the mall. Indiana has four bodyguards."

The entourage surrounded Indiana when Lane and Matt found the five having something to eat at the food court in Market Mall. Christine was wearing black pants and a blue sweater. He noted the admiring glances from a table of nearby teenaged boys who looked from Christine to Alex and back again. Then he saw Christine and Dan's eyes constantly monitoring the crowd. A passerby came within a metre of the baby stroller. Christine placed both of her hands on the stroller's handle, and Dan stood. The passerby passed on by. Dan sat. Lane thought, *Alison, you nasty, self-important, self-righteous zealot.* He said, "Anyone else want a coffee?"

"I win!" Dan threw his arms in the air.

Arthur smiled. "We had a bet going on about how long it would take before you wanted a coffee."

"I'd like a hot drink." Alex said.

Lane smiled, seeing Alex in a fleece bomber jacket zipped to the chin and leaning into Matt sitting next to her. "Warm me up." Then she looked at Lane. "Tea, please."

Lane walked over to the coffee shop, placed the orders, paid, and waited while he inhaled the aromas from the espresso machine. He looked around at the others waiting for coffee, fixing coffee, paying for coffee. A woman had her purse open, her change purse and a credit card in her left hand. Her left thumb held a Canadian passport against the change purse. Lane thought about another case.

When he returned and distributed the three drinks, Arthur asked, "What?"

Lane looked at Arthur, who held Indiana. The baby seemed content to doze in the crook of his partner's arm. "What are you asking?"

Arthur used his free hand to point at Lane. "You've got that look on your face. Either you've got indigestion or you've had some kind of epiphany about your case."

Matt said, "Looks like gas to me."

Dan said, "Or he's had one too many coffees."

Christine said, "He's always had one too many coffees!"

Alex asked, "You're on a case?"

That's when the laughter began. Then Indiana woke up and started to cry, setting off a flurry of activity around him.

✕

"What's going on here?" Arthur wore his glasses, sitting up in bed with a book on his lap.

"Could you be a bit more specific?" Lane lifted the covers, sliding in on his side of the bed.

"Matt and Alex went to a movie." Arthur took his glasses off.

"Yes. The baby is asleep, and Christine and Dan are as well." *Where is this going?*

"I'm worried about Matt, and I'm worried about what will happen when Alison gets out of jail."

"She could get six months or she could get ten years."

Arthur stuffed a bookmark in the novel. "Or she could get nothing."

Lane shrugged. "That's out of our hands — unless of course we're called to testify."

"So we just sit and wait?"

"We can't very well tell Matt and Alex not to be attracted to each other. And we can't control what my sister will do. I suspect she'll open her mouth and dig herself into a deeper hole in court, but that's really up to her. So all we can do is pick up the pieces when Alex goes home. In the meantime, the five of us will all keep Indy safe." Lane looked at the ceiling.

Arthur smiled. "Who knew breeders lived such complicated lives?"

Lane laughed.

Arthur began to chuckle. "I mean Alison fucks up her own life, and she's determined to do the same to Christine. Then Lola tries to turn Christine white so she'll be more acceptable to her country club friends. Now Matt is snuggling up to his cousin's sister. Sometimes I feel like we're preparing a real-life reality show!"

"You know this case Nigel and I are working on?"

Arthur turned to face his partner.

"A person of interest is a forty-five-year-old hairdresser who likes boys in their early teens."

"Kind of ironic when you think about it."

Lane looked at Arthur. "What do you mean?"

"Some people think we're abnormal."

chapter 9

Accused Child Abductors Remanded

Efram Milton, Alison Milton, and Lyle Pratt of Paradise, Alberta, will remain in custody until their trial dates. The three members of a polygamist community are accused of attempting to abduct an infant from the Neo-natal Intensive Care Unit at the Foothills Medical Centre. The judge agreed with the Crown Prosecutor Lilian Choi that the three pose a flight risk.

Choi said, "The accused planned to take the infant across the border and into the United States."

"I have an idea for our next move," Lane said as Nigel came into the office and hung up his winter jacket behind the door.

"I'm listening as long as it doesn't involve sending Lori back to the hair salon." Nigel sat down at his desk, rubbing his hands together, then cupping them over a pair of red ears.

"We need the driver's licence photos of Cori Pierce and her husband." Lane tapped his mouse, the fan whirring as the computer woke up.

"What for?" Nigel reached for his mouse and typed in a password.

"First we need to put them up on this page next to Peggy Carr." Lane pointed at the screen.

"Just a second." Nigel tapped his keys. "One photo is on its way. Here comes the other."

Lane downloaded the photos and put them on the screen. "We've got three suspects. We've seen two. Now let's take a look at Dr. Andrew Pierce."

"Before we go there, we need to work out some details." Nigel picked up a file from his desk.

"Like what?" *Nigel's enjoying this.*

"We need to know who we should concentrate on. These killers — and it looks like there are two — are certain to kill again."

"I was thinking that they probably have false passports but their credit cards may be legit. They might have made a mistake there. The way Lori described her, Cori strikes me as a person who likes to enjoy the spoils." Lane looked at Cori's picture on the screen.

"And I know someone who can check on that. There will be no way the Pierces will know they are suspects."

Lane said, "We risk tainting the evidence. We can't take that risk if they walk because of it."

"It's just a way to check and see if they used their credit cards while they were in New York, Toronto, or Playa del

Carmen at the time of the other murders. If we can confirm they were there, and they travelled under different names, then we will have a pretty good idea they are the ones we should be watching."

"How are you going to do this?" Lane watched Nigel flip a pencil back and forth across the knuckles of his right hand.

"I have a friend. I've known her since high school. She's very good and very discreet. That's all you need to know."

Lane lifted his eyebrows, looking at his partner.

"She got suspended from school for hacking into the school board's computer system. She still believes she was being unfairly treated by a teacher who we all knew was a misogynistic prick, but the administration wouldn't take her complaint seriously. So she got their attention. She has a very highly developed sense of right and wrong, and she sticks strictly to her laws of fairness. She did wonderful work on various websites to promote awareness on a wide range of social and environmental issues, but wouldn't hand them in for marks. She believed it was about educating people about the issues rather than self-interest. After my mom was killed, she helped me track down the assets my father hid. She did it because she believed it was the right thing to do."

Lane held up his hand. "Where do we meet her?"

"We don't." Nigel pointed at Lane. "I do." He pointed at his chest.

Lane frowned. "I need to take a look at Dr. Pierce anyway."

Nigel looked at his partner. "I've got his teaching schedule."

"How did you get that?"

Nigel rolled his eyes.

"Okay. Just don't jeopardize the investigation."

Nigel frowned. "You don't trust me?"

Lane opened his mouth to reply. *What can you say about that without putting your foot in your mouth?*

Nigel got up, grabbing his coat. "Make sure you change your clothes if you decide to go to Pierce's afternoon lecture. Maybe take a backpack and a computer to hide behind. There are one hundred thirty-two students registered in the session. Sit at the back and keep a low profile." He put on his coat and left.

×

Nigel stepped between the sliding glass doors at the Nose Hill Public Library with its red brick and ample glass. He was warmed by a blast of air, unzipping his jacket before stepping inside of the library proper.

It took a minute to find Anna at the back, sitting in a chair with a laptop on her knees. She kept her blonde hair cut short, weighed about one hundred twenty-five pounds, stood about five ten, and appeared to be an island of tranquility within the bustle of the library.

Nigel took off his coat and sat across from her. He noted the pink hand-knit mittens and toque sitting on the table next to her. She wore a pair of blue overall-style ski pants and a pink knitted sweater. He sat there for five minutes as her fingers tapped on the keyboard. He wondered about the VENEER & PLASTIC, PLASTIC & VENEER label on the back cover of her screen. She stopped, looking up. "What's up, Nelly?"

That's the way it always is with her. Ever since she found out my middle name is Evan and my initials are NEL, she calls me Nelly. To her, the joke never gets old. "Things are good, Anna. How are you?"

She looked at his hands. "You're still boxing."

He nodded.

"The risk of brain injury is substantial."

He nodded again.

"Stop."

"I need your help with a problem." Nigel leaned forward in his chair.

"Yes." Anna studied him.

"I have copies of five IDs. I need to know if any of them used a credit card near any of these three locations during specific time frames." Nigel reached into the pocket of his winter jacket, pulling out three sheets of paper.

Anna took the papers, looking at each one. "Why?"

"I need to know if we're looking at the right people."

Anna nodded. "Bad people?"

Nigel raised his eyebrows and his shoulders.

"Well?"

"They may be very bad people. You need to be very discreet."

Anna nodded, stood up, and closed her laptop, slipping it into its pink sleeve, tucking the sleeve into her backpack, and pulling on a red winter jacket. "I'm going home now. I'll phone." She picked up her mitts and toque, then walked away.

×

Lane picked up a coffee at a kiosk on the foyer on the main floor of the University of Calgary's Education Classroom Block. The architecture had a dark, mid-last-century feel. He watched young people walk past or around him without taking much notice. *They look so young!* He caught the scent of a citrus perfume, then the stronger scent of cologne. It tickled his nose, and he sneezed into the crook of his elbow.

For an instant there was quiet. People turned, noticing him in his open-necked blue shirt and black pants. Then their eyes glazed over and they turned away. Except for one young woman, who smiled. "Bless you. You're Christine's uncle."

He smiled, winking, putting his finger to his lips. She nodded, looking away. He hefted a green backpack he'd borrowed from Matt. Inside was an iPad borrowed from Dan, and a notebook and pencil he'd grabbed from his desk at work.

Lane saw a pair of young women open the door to the lecture theatre and followed them inside. He found himself at the top of steps leading to a stage and lectern. The room was brightly lit. The pair ahead of him stepped down to a middle row, sidling left to sit dead centre in the room. *They're going to be right at Dr. Pierce's eye level.* He moved left, choosing a seat in the back row behind a guy wearing a football jacket and built like Lane's stainless-steel fridge.

More people arrived and began to fill up the theatre. Lane took off his jacket, hung it on the back of his chair, and reached into the backpack for the iPad and notebook. He opened the notebook, propped up the iPad, and used the pencil to doodle ideas. From time to time he'd glance up at the clock as the theatre gradually filled. He began to shift in his seat. *I don't know if I can sit here for ninety minutes.*

On his right, a woman of Christine's age with long black hair took off her full-length black wool coat, smiling at him, then pointing at the chair between them. "Mind if I put my coat there?"

Lane nodded, smiling back. "Of course not."

"Thanks."

A tall, lanky blond-haired man of about thirty-five entered from a door at stage right. He wore a green-and-white checked shirt, tight-fitting dark-grey slacks, and brown leather shoes. He stood behind the lectern, opened a textbook, leaned to one side to turn on the microphone, tapped it, and began to speak. "Today I'll begin with a personal story, and then we'll get to work on the characteristics of bullying.

"When I was nineteen, I went into a bar in Macklin, Saskatchewan. Half an hour later a woman picked me up off the gravel in the parking lot, took me home in her Buick, and cleaned up the cuts on my face and knuckles. I remember she put a butterfly bandage here —" he pointed at his forehead "— as she told me, 'You did a dance with those two guys. A dance that meant the moment you walked in the door I knew you would end up in the parking lot with a face like this.' She was doing her doctoral research on aggressive human behaviours. I —" he pointed at his chest "— became a chapter in her dissertation."

He pressed a button. The screen behind him lit up. The cover of a book appeared. The title *Unraveling the Human Puzzle* was set above a picture of a group of human silhouettes with drinks in their hands. The black silhouettes were overlaid with white puzzle piece designs. Across the bottom of the page ran *Dr. Andrew Pierce, PhD.*

"Bullies and their prey do a kind of dance."

From the right, a hand went up. Lane spotted the back and shoulders of a man of about forty whose black hair was thin on top and grey at the sides. Lane watched Pierce, who smirked as he acknowledged the man by holding out his hand for him to speak.

The man pointed his finger at the screen. "I read the chapter, and in it you say the victim only has to realize he or she can stop the behaviours triggering the bully's actions. Isn't that a bit like blaming the victim?"

Pierce looked at the pair of young women sitting at his eye level in the centre of the room. A brief smile appeared and disappeared. He lifted his eyebrows. "All the victim need do is recognize the signs, as I needed to do before I went into the bar in Macklin and as you —" He turned to face the man who'd asked the question.

Through the microphone, Lane could hear every nuance in the professor's voice. *It's filled with contempt.*

"— need to learn. There is a dance humans do to establish a hierarchy, and you need to learn your place within the hierarchy."

One of the young women sitting in front of the professor began to laugh, covering her mouth with her hand and leaning closer to her friend. She talked behind her hand.

A broad smile profiled Pierce's whitened teeth. "Even Darwin knew that natural selection favours those at the top of the food chain rather than those at the bottom."

The ears of the man who'd asked the question turned red. Then his scalp did the same.

Lane watched the professor through narrowing eyes. He felt an inexplicable rage building. Tears formed in his eyes. He wiped at them with the index and fore fingers of his right hand. *What the hell is my problem?*

The young woman sitting next to him handed him a tissue. She leaned in close. "Pierce is such a douche."

An hour later, when Lane left the theatre, he checked his phone for messages and found one from Arthur.

×

"What?" Nigel sat across from Lane in their downtown office. The door was closed, and Lane was staring at his computer screen.

Lane shook his head. "When will your contact have the information?"

"When she's done."

Lane turned to his partner. The aftermath of rage was still in his eyes. He'd been unable to walk it off after the twenty-minute trek to where he'd parked the car. Even the minus twenty temperature and a brisk wind out of the north had failed to cool his anger to the point where he could think clearly.

Nigel's eyes opened wider. He held his hands up in mock surrender. "That's just the way she works. She's done when she's done. She lives in the basement suite of her house. Her parents live upstairs. Her mom likes to keep an eye on her."

"Her house! How does she make a living?" *Don't take it out on Nigel. He's done nothing wrong.*

"Look." Nigel leaned forward in his chair, still holding his hands up. "I don't know. She always has the latest computer, cell phone, and iPad. She's a Mac user. Won't use anything else. She always looks well groomed. She never appears interested in the opposite sex — or the same sex, for that matter. She's totally self-contained and has this compulsion to make the world a better place. I knew her when I went to junior high, but we became friends after my mom was killed. She didn't ask any questions and didn't feel sorry for me. Then she got suspended for a week. When she came back, I treated her the same way I always had. We just became friends. We hung out together. She helped me out with some stuff. What's got you so pissed off anyway?"

"Pierce." Lane looked at the big screen and grabbed the mouse, highlighting the professor's name, then enlarging his driver's licence photo. "And my sister."

"What did Pierce do?"

Lane took a long slow breath. "He was giving a lecture on the dynamics of bullying. This guy asked a question Pierce didn't like, so Pierce belittled the guy in front of the class."

"That's all?" Nigel looked sideways at Lane.

Lane looked at Nigel, and his partner paled. "It was the way he did it. I can't explain it. He's giving a lecture to young people who will be teachers, and at the same time he's bullying one of his students. It was the voice he used. The way he did it to impress a couple of the young women in class. The way some of them laughed. It was..."

"Fucked up."

Lane almost laughed. "What's a douche?"

"What?"

"Douche. The young woman next to me called Pierce a douche. What is it?"

"Someone who comes across being all cool and tailor made, but is a real self-centred asshole underneath."

"Tailor made. That's it. All of his clothes were tailor made. Even his shoes. How could he afford all of that? I mean, professors aren't paid *that* well." Lane looked at his partner.

"And what about your sister?"

"She's back, and now she's got some money behind her. Some organization called the Canadian Celestial Institute. I know she'll use any means possible to punish Christine. She'll do whatever she thinks is necessary to take Indiana away." Lane looked back at the screen, shaking his head. "And I can't do a damn thing about it because Alison thinks she has God on her side."

But I can stop her. Nigel stood up. "It's quittin' time."

Lane nodded. "Okay."

Nigel handed Lane his jacket. Lane took it, walking out the door. Nigel hung back. "See you tomorrow." He waited until Lane was out of sight, then took out his phone and typed a text message. "We need another meet."

✕

Anna was waiting for him at eight thirty. She sat in the same chair at the Nose Hill Public Library. She was tapping the screen of her iPad with the forefinger of her right hand. Beside her, the pink tablet cover had VENEER & PLASTIC, PLASTIC & VENEER written across it.

Nigel stood beside her.

Without looking up, she said, "I planned on doing the job later tonight."

"I have another job for you. Remember how you got twenty percent for finding and transferring the funds my dad hid?" Nigel asked.

Anna nodded.

"I need you to transfer some money. This time, you do what you want with it. Just get it out of the hands of the people who have it."

"I need a reason."

"They're trying to take a baby away from his mother."

"What's the mother like?" Anna asked.

"She's the niece of a friend. She's African Canadian. The people who want the baby think my friend's a bad influence because he's gay."

"Is he?"

"Is he what?"

"A bad influence?"

"Just the opposite."

Anna nodded. "Got the information?"

Nigel handed her a sheet of paper. Anna took it, reading the details. "I'll work on it." She slid the iPad in its cover.

He pointed at the words written across the pink. "What's that mean?"

She smiled. "You'll figure it out." Anna pulled on her jacket, wrapped a scarf around her neck, and walked toward the door.

✕

Lane sat in the family room in one of the easy chairs. Dan sat next to Christine on the couch while she fed Indiana. Alex sat on the hearth with her back to the gas fireplace. Matt sat nearby. Arthur nestled in another easy chair. He was trying to watch celebrities dance, but Christine insisted the sound be muted. Alex pointed at the screen, putting her hand over her mouth. A blonde-haired celebrity dancer had a blacked-out breast. It had popped out of her low-cut sequined costume.

Dan said, "I hope her partner doesn't get hit by that thing. It could be a career ender."

Christine elbowed him.

"Ouch." Dan rubbed his ribs.

"Why don't you two go out now, and we'll watch Indiana?" Alex had her hands tucked around her elbows.

Christine shook her head. "I'm not leaving him alone."

Lane looked at Arthur, who was watching Christine intently.

Matt asked, "You think we won't take good care of him?"

Dan looked at Christine, who was staring at Indiana. "That's not it at all. We got news today. Alison is getting financial support from some organization so she can hire a lawyer and try to take Indy."

Lane watched Christine holding her son. *Damn it, Alison. Don't you know you're pushing her away rather than bringing her closer?*

chapter 10

Institute Promises to Pay Legal Fees for Trio Accused of Abduction

A representative of the Canadian Celestial Institute says his organization stands behind the actions of three people charged with attempted child abduction.

At a news conference on Tuesday, Orson Nelson announced the Institute will be funding legal defence costs for Efram Milton, Alison Milton, and Lyle Pratt, all currently in custody for an alleged abduction attempt earlier this month.

"These folks were clearly acting in the best interests of the child when they entered the Foothills Medical Centre," says Nelson, the self-declared president of the CCI.

According to a statement on its website, the CCI "defends the right to religious freedom as set out in the Canadian Charter of Rights and the Constitution of the United States."

Story continues page B3

"Would you be willing to give Donna a call this morning?" Lane sat to one side of Lori's desk. He leaned forward, setting a cup of tea next to her phone.

Lori took the tea and sipped, looking over Lane's shoulder. "Nigel will be angry with me."

"And me." Lane took the last sip from his coffee, tossing the paper cup in the trash.

"She's not a suspect?" Lori sat up, crossing one leg over the other. She wore a pair of tan leather boots reaching just below the knee of her black slacks.

"What do you think?" Lane stuck his hands under his armpits. His fingers were still cold from the walk from the LRT station.

"I'm not in your line of work, but —" Lori looked directly at Lane "— she doesn't seem like she's hiding anything or even capable of subterfuge. The impression I get of Donna is what you see is what you get."

"Then the next step is for me to talk with her, but it would help if I had you along to smooth the way."

Lori frowned. "I hadn't realized you could be so calculating."

"It's called catching a killer before more people are hurt." Lane wondered about the defensive tone in his voice.

"Just don't be going over to the dark side. There's been enough of that around here already." She reached into her purse, pulled out a business card, held it up, and waved him away with her free hand. "Haven't you got work to do?"

Lane sprang up, stepping into his office. He sat down, started up his computer, and looked over the ever-expanding map of details connected to the Randall case. He began separate maps for Peggy Carr, Cori and Andrew Pierce, David and Melissa Randall, and Megan and Doug Newsome. *Right now, Cori and Andrew are persons of interest. This needs to be ready if Nigel comes up with some evidence proving I'm wrong.*

My gut is telling me I'm right about the Pierces.

Lori stuck her head in the door twenty minutes later. She wore a red wool coat with its lapels stuck up under her ears. The hem of the coat reached to the tops of her tan boots. "Nigel's still at the doctor. Donna is at her house. She's waiting to talk with a contractor. She says she'll be there for an hour, maybe two. We need to go now."

Lori began doing up her buttons, then taking black leather mitts out of a voluminous black leather purse.

Lane logged off, got up, and grabbed his winter coat.

They shivered as the Chev's heater blasted the windshield with cold air. Lane tried to breathe out of the corners of his mouth. Otherwise, his breath would fog up the inside of the glass, and they'd have to wait longer for the car to warm up. He looked right, seeing Lori's passenger window fogging up. *Why does the woman's side of a vehicle always turn opaque?*

The tires rolled like squares until the corners warmed up. He watched the engine temperature as they drove along 6th Avenue. It nudged up above cold, beginning a slow climb as they drove west, then up the hill along Bow Trail beside the LRT tracks. By the time they reached Shaganappi Golf Course, the inside of the car was comfortably lukewarm, and they were able to open their coats.

"So, if you can stop talking, maybe I can get a word in." Lori pointed at a coyote running across the snow-covered fairway. "Looks like he's not feeling the cold."

"Sorry. I'm trying to figure out what to do about my sister and her gang." Lane glanced at the coyote as it ran with its nose out front and the tip of its tail out back.

"Doesn't she have fifteen other kids to raise?"

"I don't know how many kids Alison has. But I wish she would leave Christine alone. She had the kid excommunicated and washed her hands of her. I don't get why she has to keep punishing her daughter when she's cut her off." Lane passed a fourteen-storey high-rise, following the curve of the road when they began a gentle climb toward Coach Hill.

"Because Christine was supposed to be learn her lesson. Instead Christine is going to school, she has a son, she's doing just fine, and Alison can't stand it because Christine was supposed to come crawling back. Alison wants control over Christine. But you and I both know that isn't going to happen, so Alison has to punish her and you —" she poked Lane in the arm "— by trying to take Indiana away."

"You think that's what it is?" Lane looked right at Lori.

She nodded. "And because Alison is afraid."

"That too?"

"Sure. She's afraid of anything that doesn't fit into her narrow little view of life, and you, my friend, definitely don't fit into her idea of what she would call God's plan."

"What does she think should happen?"

Lori laughed. "You should be damned for your lifestyle, and Christine should be living a miserable life as punishment for her defiance. The opposite is happening, and it drives Alison crazy."

Lane shook his head as they climbed the steep grade up to the top of Coach Hill, then turned right into a residential area. "What makes you so sure that's what she's doing?"

"My mother was the same way." Lori turned to watch the numbers on the houses. "Donna said it was a brown two-storey with a couple of big evergreens out front."

Lane spotted the house and parked behind a red pickup truck. "Maybe the contractor is already here." He shut off the engine. They pulled on gloves and mitts, stepping out of the car and doing up their jackets.

"Shit, that wind is cold." Lori led the way to the side of the two-car garage so they could get out of the wind. "Donna said to go around back to the shop." They walked along a freshly shovelled sidewalk and around the corner of the house.

"Hang on." Lane touched her elbow. He stepped into the snow at the side of the walk, walked in front of her, and promptly ran into a man wearing overlarge winter boots, tan cotton overalls, an open green military jacket, a toque, and a week's worth of beard.

"Sorry, man. You here to see Donna?" the man asked.

"Yes." Lane stepped back and onto Lori's toe.

"Hey! These are my new boots." Lori's voice held the hint of a smile.

The contractor stepped around them. "I wouldn't go in there just yet. She's having an argument with her kid."

Lane turned the corner and into the wind. It cut into the flesh of his nose, chin, and cheeks. He pulled up the collar of his jacket to cover his ears, turning his back to the wind. He saw Lori tuck her head down inside of her red coat. He knocked, then opened the back door.

Donna stood inside. "You are not going back to playing hockey with your team." She wore a black dress, black tights, and a high-stepping pair of black boots. She faced a twelve-year-old boy with black hair and a white plastic brace around his neck. He wore a blue T-shirt and red sweat pants with HAWKS in white letters down one leg.

"Mom! My friends are on the team!"

"How many of those friends came to see you in the hospital? How many of those friends know you have a cracked vertebra in your neck? How close did you come to being in a wheelchair? You're not playing fucking contact hockey anymore!"

"I wanna play in the NHL!"

Lane and Lori could hear the exasperation in Donna's voice. "Fuck the NHL! If you survive to make it to the NHL, then what? What kind of life is that for anyone? They buy and trade you like a fucking slave! You want to be a slave?"

"Mom! You're such a drama queen! That's not what it's like!"

"Look, Hansen, when you're healed up, maybe in the fall, you can play volleyball at school."

"Volleyball is for douches!"

"Well at least you'll be a live douche who can use both arms and both legs!"

"I don't care what you say! I'm gonna play hockey!" Hansen turned, stepped through the open side door, and slammed it.

Donna took a step toward the door and stopped. She looked at herself in the full-length mirror. It stood in front of one of the black chairs her customers would eventually sit in. She shook her head, taking a deep breath.

Lori said, "Maybe this isn't such a good time."

This could be a very good time. Donna is upset and more likely to say whatever is on her mind.

Lori looked at the snow on her boots.

Donna turned, glaring at them, her back rigid with anger.

She's wondering what else could happen today. Lane stepped inside, closing the door. They stamped their feet on a left-over patch of carpet. The room smelled of fresh paint and the adhesive used to glue linoleum to the floor. Lane looked around at two new sinks for washing hair, two new black chairs for customers to sit in. Both chairs faced large, well-lit mirrors. A hair dryer sat above another chair along the far wall. The room was painted in tasteful colours. He said, "It looks like it's almost ready."

"This is Detective Lane." Lori pointed at him as she took off her gloves.

Lane offered his hand. Donna shook it. He felt the heat of her anger in the fierceness of her grip. She turned to Lori. "You're a cop."

"Actually I'm his secretary." Lori smiled, pulling off her gloves and opening her coat.

Donna shook her head, chuckling. "They've been doing budget cuts again?"

Lori smiled. "Somebody has to keep the boys on their best behaviour."

Lane unzipped his jacket. "I asked her to go and see you. We're investigating the Randall and Newsome murders."

"And you think I killed them?" Donna crossed her arms under her breasts, tapping the toe of her boot.

"Did you?" *Let's go with this and see where it leads.*

Donna cocked her head to the right. "The night it happened I was in Emergency with my son." She looked at Lori. "You got kids?"

"Three." Lori's fingers struggled with a stubborn button.

"You?" Donna looked at Lane.

"A niece and a nephew." Lane watched Donna warily.

"And a baby. Don't forget him." Lori turned to Lane. "They all live with him and his partner."

Donna studied Lane for a minute. "How come they're living with you?"

"It's a long story." *This isn't going the way I'd hoped.*

Donna waited.

What the hell. "My nephew's mom died of cancer, and his dad started a new family. Matt needed a place to live. Then my niece ran away from Paradise."

"That's the polygamist community near the US border, right?" Donna asked.

Lane nodded. *Don't push her. Just take your time.*

"They tried to take her baby from the hospital?"

"That's right."

"Read about that in the paper. I have a sister who went all religious on us. Married a guy who likes to use the Bible to keep her under his thumb. Is it like that?" Donna asked.

"More or less." *Don't say it.* "My sister is pretty fucked up." *Why did you go ahead and say that?*

Donna nodded.

"Why are you moving out of Platinum?" Lori asked.

Donna considered the question for a minute. "I don't like working at a place where a forty-five-year-old woman preys on boys a little older than my son."

"And?" Lane asked.

Donna looked past Lane into her backyard. "I get a bad feeling."

"Anything specific?" Lane asked.

"Yesterday Cori's husband arrived to pick her up. He was driving a brand-new BMW. Sometimes he picks her up in an Aston Martin. When the roads are really bad, he drives a Porsche Cayenne."

"You sure know your cars," Lane said.

Donna laughed. "I have two sons. It's what they like to talk about."

"Anything else?"

"They live in a palace in Mount Royal."

Lane waited.

"I work in the same shop as she does. My husband has a good job. We're doing okay and we can afford this place. Cori likes to brag that when they go to buy a car, the salesmen are there to open their doors when they arrive. She says it's because they've bought five vehicles and always pay cash. Then she has high-end customers who keep getting killed. Melissa Randall invited Cori to a party a couple of months ago. Now Melissa is dead."

"What are you saying?" Lane asked.

"That something stinks. I've been working with her for a few months, and I get this creepy feeling. That's what I'm saying." Donna raised her eyebrows, let her arms drop to her sides, and shrugged. "It's fucked up."

Ten minutes later the car was warming up again while Lane drove them back down the hill toward the river valley. The sun was bright, surrounded by a sundog's halo.

Lori turned to him. "What did you bring me along for?"

"I thought I might need an icebreaker. Donna might have been angry because I sent you to her under the pretence of getting your hair cut. People react in all sorts of ways to being a suspect. She's smart and way ahead of us. She told us what she thought instead of what she thought we wanted to hear. Not all interviews go that well." Lane shoulder checked, easing around a small silver car doing ten kilometres under the speed limit. A person of indeterminate sex wearing a black toque drove staring straight ahead.

"Got a death grip on the wheel." Lori watched the driver as they passed. "Winter just freaks some people out."

"I thought you hated winter." Lane checked in his mirror before moving back into the right lane.

"I hate the icy roads." Her phone rang and she reached into her purse. "Hello, Arthur. Your policeman is right here with me."

Lane smiled.

Lori said, "Arthur says Thomas Pham phoned to say he'll represent you."

"How much?"

"Your honey asks how much?" Lori listened for a minute. "That much!" She turned to Lane and started laughing.

×

This is Shazia Wajdan outside Calgary Police Service headquarters, where Chief Jim Simpson finds himself under intense pressure. The recent murders of Robert and Elizabeth Randall and of Megan and Douglas Newsome have drawn negative attention on the Service for the potential wrongful arrest and conviction of a homeless man named Byron Thomas. Thomas is currently serving twenty-five years for murder. It now appears Thomas was convicted for a crime he did not commit.

CUT TO DETECTIVE NIGEL LI, CALGARY POLICE SERVICE
"Mr. Thomas confessed to the murder of Irena and Rodney Wiley three years ago. Physical evidence linked Mr. Thomas to the crime scene. At the time Thomas was homeless and suffering from mental health issues."

Police sources say the Wiley, Randall, and Newsome murders may be linked to at least two other homicides. But Chief Simpson is downplaying the possibility.

CUT TO CHIEF JIM SIMPSON, CALGARY POLICE SERVICE
"All avenues must be explored. It is our job to protect the citizens of Calgary and arrest those responsible for these murders."

The Newsomes' deaths marked the sixth murder of a prominent Calgarian couple in only three years.

Shazia Wajdan, CBC News, Calgary.

Lane sat at the conference table with Thomas Pham, Arthur, Christine, Dan, and Indiana, who slept in his car seat next to his mother and father. The sunlight from the south-facing windows made it feel as if, at least in this room, winter was under control.

Tommy, as always, was dressed elegantly in a navy-blue suit and a red tie. Lane noticed there was a little grey at the edges of his thick black hair. Tommy was also getting a bit round in the face. *I heard you got married last year.*

Tommy looked at the notepad in front of him. "Just a moment. Before we begin, I've asked my legal secretary to join us."

A moment later there was a knock at the door and a solidly built woman with red hair, an emerald-green jacket, a white blouse, and black wool slacks walked in, sitting next to Tommy. "Hello. My name is Sylvia. Tommy speaks well of you. He says you're part of the family."

Lane saw the jade elephant nestled between her breasts, and the engagement and wedding rings on her left hand. He looked at Tommy's hand, noting the wedding bands matched.

Christine opened the conversation. "My mother tried to take my baby away, and now she's got the CCI involved."

"The Canadian Celestial Institute?" Tommy asked.

Christine nodded. "It's run by one of Milton's polygamist buddies."

"Polygamists?" Sylvia asked.

"Yes. I lived in the Paradise community with my mother for eight years. I was on one of their fuck charts before I left." Christine glanced at Dan.

A shudder worked its way around Sylvia's shoulders. She looked sideways at Tommy, mouthing the words *fuck chart.* Tommy nodded to her.

He looks like he might be looking forward to meeting Milton in court, Lane thought as he turned to his niece. "You told me a different story."

Christine turned to him. "I didn't tell you all of the story. I left just like I told you. I just never told you about the chart."

"Are you willing to testify in court about the chart?" Tommy asked.

"Will it help me keep Indiana?" Christine asked.

"Your mother will probably say she believes the child is in danger of being neglected or abused. Your testimony about your name on such a chart will raise doubts about the safety of your mother's home. Is there anyone who can corroborate your statement?" Tommy looked at Sylvia.

"I don't know. It's a closed community. The woman who left at the same time I did might testify. Then again, she might not. The last I heard, some of her children were still in Paradise." Christine shook her head. "Even after you leave, they have the ability to intimidate you by threatening to punish the people remaining in the community or preventing them from communicating with you."

"That may work for us, actually." Tommy tore a piece of yellow paper from his pad. "Would you write down the name of the woman who left with you, and the names of any other individuals who might be able to support your testimony? Were any other forms of abuse prevalent during your time there?"

"Yes. But the thing is —" Christine looked sideways at Lane and Arthur "— I had to create a diversion so that I could escape Paradise."

"Diversion?" Tommy's eyes narrowed.

Lane noticed Sylvia leaning in closer as she waited for Christine to continue.

"I set one of the houses on fire so we could get away." Christine looked at the ceiling.

"Was anyone hurt as a result of the fire?" Tommy asked.

"I don't think so. The place was empty."

"No charges were ever laid. I checked," Lane said.

Tommy made a note on his pad. "Still…"

"Her mother can use it against her?" Arthur asked.

Alison thinks God is on her side. She'll use it, Lane thought.

"We'll see. I just like to know everything there is to know so I can prepare for any and all eventualities." Tommy sat back.

"What I did…." Christine faltered. "Will it mean they can take Indy from me?"

Indiana farted. Lane looked over at the baby, who smiled. A tiny fist appeared next to his cheek.

"It appears your son isn't worried, and is perhaps even a bit dismissive of the possibility." Tommy smiled. "He may have a point. They attempted to kidnap your child. I suspect they will be so busy defending themselves that any attempt to discredit you will only make our case stronger."

Dan asked, "Would it help if we were married?"

"Will you talk with her? Christine listens to you." Arthur stood next to Lane at the front door.

"What happened?" Lane bent to unlace his boots.

"She thinks she's going to lose Indiana." There was emotion in Arthur's voice, and his hands shook as he spoke.

Lane straightened, slipping out of his boots and taking off his coat. He took Arthur's hand. "Alison's only weapon is fear. We have documentation signed by Alison stating she has no interest in raising her daughter. We have witnesses to say she excommunicated her daughter and cut Christine off from her family. And for four years she has not contacted her daughter. There is also the issue of the Lost Boys, who will be brought up if this ever goes to trial."

"Can you tell her that?" Arthur put his hand on Lane's shoulder, steering him toward the top of the stairs leading to the family room.

Lane felt almost overwhelming dread. *What happens if I'm wrong?* He nearly missed the top step. Grabbing the railing, Lane closed his eyes and took a breath, then made his way down to the oak hardwood floor of the family room. Christine sat in the oversized chocolate-brown leather chair with Indiana asleep in her arms.

Lane heard movement on his left. He turned to see Dan on the couch. His eyes were wide, underlined with fatigue. Dan nodded.

"Just tell me." Christine stared straight ahead at the muted TV. "How long do I have with Indy?"

"The rest of your life. He will always be your son." Lane sat down on the arm of the chair. *Christine, you could use a bath.* The scent was a warning bell in Lane's mind.

"But how long will he be with me?" Christine turned to look at her son.

"Two things. And I want you to remember them when Indy has his first temper tantrum. And I want you to go and soak in the bath while I hold the baby." Lane put his hand on her shoulder.

Christine's eyes were overflowing with tears. "Why does she want him and not me?"

Indiana brought his knees up. He grimaced, beginning to cry. Christine put him on her shoulder.

"Your son may be trying to tell you something," Lane said.

"What's that?" Christine asked.

"He needs you. And don't forget about the two things. Alison is the one charged with child abduction. And Tommy is the best. That's why we hired him."

"But they say they have the right to take him away."

Lane took a long breath. "They can say what they like because it's all they can do. They talk because they have no other recourse, and they've proved they think they have the right to take the law into their own hands."

"You don't know how they operate." Christine rubbed Indiana's back with her right hand.

Lane lifted his eyebrows. "I don't?"

Dan began to laugh, and Christine smiled. "I'm scared."

"Maybe Alison and Milton should be scared. Tommy can be ferocious. This is a case he can really get his teeth into. I'm beginning to think the CCI and Milton have bitten off more than they can chew."

chapter 11

"How'd it go with the doctor?" Lane asked when Nigel walked into the office and sat down at his desk.

"I had an MRI. The doctor told me to stop boxing or I'm risking permanent brain damage." Nigel looked at Lane.

It sounds like he wants my advice. "What do you think?" *Coward! Just tell him.*

"I know that the hammering —" he tapped the side of his skull "— isn't healthy. I was hoping you would know why I do it. You're good at figuring out motives."

Shit! Lane looked at his partner, wondering what would come of what he was about to say. "You probably won't like it."

Nigel nodded, holding the palm of his right hand open for his partner, indicating Lane should go ahead.

"It's something you probably need to figure out for yourself."

"Please, just say it."

Lane inhaled. *Don't do it!* "I think you feel responsible for what happened to your mother, and your emotions say you need to be punished even though you know —" Lane tapped the side of his head "— in your mind you are not responsible."

Nigel stood up, catching the tops of his thighs on the underside of his desk. He howled with pain.

Lane recoiled at the sound, the wail of an animal whose wound is exposed after being protected by layers of scar tissue.

Lori opened the door seconds later. "What the hell is going on here?" She spotted a doubled-over Nigel, turned her anger on Lane. "What did you do?"

Nigel rubbed his thighs. "Nothing. He did nothing."

Lori looked at Lane, then back at Nigel. "Bullshit." She crossed her arms, waiting.

Nigel got up, grabbed his coat, and walked around his desk. "I need some air."

Lori looked at Lane and shook her head. "What did you say to him?"

✕

"Hello? Detective Lane? This is Donna Liu."

Lane looked across at the people sitting on the C-Train. One was reading a book. Another was listening to music. A man leaned against the glass and napped. The air smelled of warm clothing, sweat, and electric heat. "Hello." Lane stared at his reflection in the glass. The buildings of the University of Calgary formed a backdrop.

"Can you talk?"

Lane heard the hollow sounds of road traffic, guessing Donna was in her car. "I can't but you can."

"Shit! Sorry, some guy just cut me off. That was close."

Lane waited.

"There was talk at work today. Another of the Nine Bottles is going to have a party. Well, it's five bottles now. Or is it four? Anyway, there's a party at Brockington House. Can you believe she has a title for her house? I can get back to you with more details if you like."

"Yes, please. How's your son?"

"The same. Talk with you in a day or two. Bye."

✕

About a kilometre away, Nigel walked into the Nose Hill Public Library. At night, the blast of warm air at the entrance created a bit of fog as winter elbowed its way through the doors. He stepped through the second set of doors, removing cap and gloves, unzipping his coat, and looking for Anna.

What Lane said made you angry because it was the truth. You asked him to tell you, and he did. Get over it.

He found her standing over a man who had made the unfortunate mistake of sitting in Anna's chair. She wore a faux-leather fighter pilot's helmet, a pair of steampunk glasses with red and violet lenses, mitts, and a brown faux-leather bomber jacket. Anna leaned over the arm of the chair, breathing on the man's head. "Is there a problem?" he asked.

"You're sitting in my chair." Anna's volume made several people turn to look. She flicked down a violet lens overtop the red one.

A few regulars stared angrily at the man. He frowned, looking at his book, then settled deeper into the chair.

Anna leaned closer, took off her mitt, and hung it between two fingers. She brushed the mitt against the man's left ear. He swatted at it, but she was too quick. She brushed his ear again. He swatted, missing.

"Okay! Shit! Have the chair!" He stood up — all six foot four and two hundred ninety pounds of him — grabbed his coat, and stormed off.

Anna took off her coat, helmet, and mitts. The she pulled her laptop computer out from under her white cable turtleneck. She sat down and opened the laptop.

Nigel took off his coat and sat across from her. *No need to mention what just happened. She'll already have moved on. Just get right to the point.* "What have you got?"

Anna looked up at Nigel, setting the laptop on the round table in front of her and pointing at the screen. "Milton has fourteen bank accounts in the US, Canada, and the Grand Cayman Islands. He also has three insurance policies and five numbered companies. Then there are the businesses."

Nigel got up, walked to her side of the table, and crouched beside her. She had all the information itemized on a spreadsheet. "Any idea on the total amount stashed away?"

"Twenty-seven point six seven million using today's rates of exchange. He uses mostly US and Canadian dollars, but a few of the investments are in gold."

Nigel looked at the spreadsheet. *It's all there.*

"Not surprising when you realize he has a very large and very cheap labour force at his disposal."

"He does have that."

"What's the baby's mom like?" Anna asked.

"Young. It's her first child. She escaped the polygamist community and was excommunicated."

"Then why do they want her baby?"

Nigel shook his head. "Maybe her mother wants to punish her some more for not being obedient. Obedience is a big thing for the women. I think it's called being sweet. Apparently it all started when Christine cut her hair short. That was a big deal for her mother."

Anna nodded. "What does the baby look like?"

"I've only seen pictures, but he has lots of black hair and brown eyes."

"Olson."

"What?" *Where is she going with this?*

"The alias on the passport. The birthdates are the same. The last name is Olson on the false passport, but not on the credit cards. Ditto Williams. Not very imaginative."

"We're talking the killers now?"

Anna nodded.

"Thanks. Now I can check the passenger lists."

"You have to see this video. It's a baby laughing." Anna didn't wait for him to respond. She tapped the track pad. A full-screen video of a round, laughing baby in diapers came into focus. Anna laughed and heads turned. Nigel heard the echo of her laughter bouncing off the walls and the ceiling. He was unable to stop smiling.

✕

"Olson? You're joking?" Lane talked on the phone as he sat upstairs on the couch. All was quiet at home, at least for the moment.

"No joke. The names match flights to New York, Toronto, and Cancun. Olson and Williams were there at the time of each of the murders."

"You sound tired."

"I am."

I need to apologize. "I'm sorry for what I said."

"I've been thinking about that."

"And?" *Just listen. Let him talk!*

"You might be right." Nigel hung up.

Lane got up, went down the stairs to the family room and then down into the basement office where he sat down, logged on, and typed an e-mail message.

Keely,

Hope you and Dylan are surviving the winter and enjoying yourselves.

I was hoping you could help with a case. We have a male and a female who may have false passports. I don't want them to be aware we are taking a close look at them. Their names are Andrew and Cori Pierce. Aliases are Clayton Olson and Karly A. Williams.

Our investigation is leading us to believe the couple may be linked to a series of homicides. Are you able to confirm they have travelled under two or more separate identities?

Christine's baby is home and doing well.

Say hello to Dylan for me.

Lane

chapter 12

Institute Backs Out of Defence for Accused Abductors

Orson Nelson, president of the Canadian Celestial Institute, says his organization is no longer able to defend Efram Milton, Alison Milton, and Lyle Pratt against charges of attempted child abduction.

In explaining this change of position on Thursday, Nelson said, "I have asked the RCMP to initiate a criminal investigation into the theft of money from the CCI defence fund."

Nelson spoke from his home in Paradise, Alberta. Paradise is the polygamist community to which the three accused belong.

The CCI President was not specific about the amount of money missing but says it is "significant."

"What's up with you today?" Lori pointed at Lane's cloth-ing. He wore a thick blue cotton shirt with a black T-shirt underneath, and blue jeans. "I almost didn't recognize you." She pointed at her tan leather boots reaching almost to her knees. "You need a pair of these if you want to fit in at the U of C."

"I don't think I'm fooling anyone when I pretend to be a student. Still, I need to keep an eye on Professor Pierce." Lane glanced to his left at his red backpack.

"You're taking a long, hard look at the him."

He nodded. "I have to turn off the ringer on my phone while I'm in class. Would you text me if Keely or Nigel wants to get in touch?"

Lori reached out, putting her hand on his elbow. "Be careful with Cori and her professor. Watching Cori operate made the hair on the back of my neck start doing a tango. If you're right about them, they'll be like that other guy."

"Moreau?" Lane reached for his coat.

"That's the one. Charming. Lethal. Good at fooling almost everyone."

"I try not to make any assumptions or reach conclusions early on. Still, I think you're correct. Indications are pointing that way." He leaned over to pick up the backpack.

"So you trust my gut?"

"Sometimes my gut is exactly what gets me looking at a suspect. The feeling that something isn't quite right. The feeling you need to keep your guard up, that you can't turn your back on a person." Lane hooked the backpack over his shoulder. "How do I look?"

Lori reached out, adjusting his collar. "Have a good day at school."

Lane laughed out loud.

"Why isn't Nigel doing this job? He's much more likely to pass as a student than you."

"He's tracking down passports. And, at least for the time being, I'd like to keep him away from these two."

"Bad karma?"

Lane leaned his head right, then left. "Something like that. I think Andrew Pierce might remind Nigel of his father and cloud his judgement."

"He's having a rough go with this one."

She's noticed it, too. "From the very first day we went to the scene."

Lori nodded. "Scars."

"What's that?"

"Just like you and me. He's got scars."

Lane sat in the back row of the main-floor lecture theatre at the University of Calgary's education building. Thankfully, the massive man-spreading football player liked to sit in the same place in the second from last row. Lane crouched behind him. He sipped from the coffee he'd bought at the kiosk in the foyer, taking notes with his right hand, glancing at the iPad for any incoming messages.

"Street smarts. There's a difference between street smarts and the kind of intelligence measured by standardized tests."

Lane looked at Pierce, who stood behind the lectern. He wore a black shirt, black jeans, and a pair of black cowboy boots. The same pair of young women sat below Lane and at eye level with Pierce. Lane noted Pierce still looked their way when he talked. "One of the guys I went to high school with was of below-average IQ. He's a millionaire today, because he has street smarts."

Lane wrote IQ in his notebook, circling it.

"Of course, standardized tests measure higher-level thought processes and are a powerful tool for the assessment of student abilities."

Lane heard absolute certainty in the professor's voice. *It's a weakness. He believes he is smarter than anyone here.*

There was a sigh from the girls down front when the man with the thinning-on-top black hair, who'd asked a question the other day, raised his hand.

Pierce turned his back on the man. "Standardized tests are meticulously researched and continuously refined."

Balding man spoke. "They are called street smarts, after all. And why, if standardized tests are meticulously researched, do they need to be refined?"

The two girls near the front turned, shaking their heads at the man who asked the question.

Lane looked at the man, who blushed as he spotted their reaction. He had an old-style winter jacket tucked in behind him and, as he leaned back, a feather puffed up out of the tired fabric.

Pierce turned toward the man. Lane saw the man inhale.

The woman beside Lane shook her head. It was the same woman with long black hair who had sat near Lane the day before. Again she had set her black wool jacket on the chair between them. Today, she wore a blue turtleneck rolled up under her chin.

Pierce said, "There is considerable scientific research supporting the efficacy of standardized tests."

Bald man said, "There is also considerable research to suggest standardized tests are only accurate indicators of the size of an individual's house. Have you read the research by Alfie Kohn?"

"Yes, I have." Pierce's tone was condescending. His face reddened.

Lane saw heads turning back and forth between Pierce and the man. Balding man said, "Then you must know there's considerable evidence suggesting conclusions contrary to the point of view you are presenting."

"And you have a PhD in statistics?" Pierce asked.

"A PhD is required before an individual is allowed to think for himself?"

"That's exactly what it means!" Pierce pointed at the man.

"Bullshit!" The woman next to Lane was standing, pointing at Pierce. "The last time I checked, education is intended to open minds rather than close them."

Pierce looked from the man to the woman. The surprise on his face transformed into rage. He pointed at the man and then the woman. "The pair of you are colluding! I can see it. You don't know who you're dealing with! What you're up against!"

"Is that a threat?" The woman put her fists on her hips.

"It's whatever you want it to be." Pierce folded up his materials, turned right, walked across the stage, and kicked the side door open. It bounced off the wall, slamming him into the doorframe on the rebound.

Lane touched the woman's elbow, and she turned on him. He held his hands palm up. She looked down at him with her fists at her sides. Lane saw the white of her knuckle bones. He said, "I have a question for you."

She took a breath. "What?"

"What made you stand up and speak out?"

"You mean you can't see it?"

Lane waited.

"There's something wrong with him. He's the last person who should be teaching us how to be teachers."

Lane kept his tone neutral. "How do you know?"

"I just know." She wiped away tears. "I just know."

✕

"What does this mean?" Christine wore a T-shirt and red flannel pants. She handed Lane a newspaper article as he stepped out of his shoes at the front door.

Lane took the paper in one hand, shook his other hand out of the sleeve of his winter jacket, then switched hands to repeat the process. Christine took his coat. Lane read the article. "The missing money makes me wonder."

"About what?" Christine leaned against the wall.

Lane moved into the living room, sitting in the easy chair. It felt warm against his back. "About what happened to the money. Do you believe Orson Nelson?"

Christine nodded. "He's a friend of Milton and Lyle Pratt. The three of them were always meeting about one thing or another. I often heard them talking about lying for the Lord." She sat down on the couch, holding the article in her left hand.

Lane looked at her.

"You know, lying to protect polygamy, religion, themselves."

"So, you think Nelson is lying?" Lane felt his cheeks warming up after the forty-minute walk home from the LRT station.

"I don't know. I'm just worried about Indiana and what my mother is up to."

Lane leaned his head back, closing his eyes. "I can see two possible scenarios. Nelson is lying to help Alison play the victim. Or something else is going on because money disappeared from the account. The fact that he won't disclose how much is missing is also telling. Either way, Tommy Pham is quite capable of protecting you and Indiana."

"How long will my mother be in jail if she's convicted?"

Lane opened his eyes when he heard the despair in Christine's voice. *This is a no-win situation for you.* "I'd expect it could be anywhere from time served to five years. You don't want her to go to prison?"

Christine shrugged. "I know it's crazy. She's my mom. I don't want her to be in jail. But I don't want us to be in this prison either." She looked around the living room. "I'm always afraid when we leave the house. Always worried when someone comes to the door."

Lane leaned forward. *What do I say to her? Your mother is mentally ill? You'll never be free of her?* "How many adults live in this house?"

"Five. Six." Christine sat back in the couch.

"That's the number of people who will fight to protect Indiana. Not everyone has a family like that. I like our odds."

Later that night, while he lay awake and Arthur snored, Lane thought, *What's going on with the CCI's money? There's something I'm missing here.* He closed his eyes until the image of David Randall with the back of his head blown away made him open them again.

chapter 13

Red Cross Rejoices at Abnormal Influx of Donations

A massive influx of small donations has provided the Calgary Red Cross with a total of more than two million dollars.

Red Cross spokesperson Mary Latourneau confirmed the anomaly. "It seems many of our regular donors decided to make donations to the disaster relief fund. It's unusual for so many people to make contributions all at once, but we're grateful."

Red Cross funds will be directed toward emergency relief operations around the globe.

"That's for sure." Nigel lifted his chin, looking ahead as he drove along Memorial Drive. On their left, the Bow River was a glittering toy box of ice blocks pointed this way and that. Here and there open patches of water created whispery clouds.

Lane saw the pickup in front of them. It was silvery blue with a round white diesel fuel tank at the front of the box and WIDE ASS painted in white across the tailgate. There were four wheels on the truck's rear axle. A chrome monkey sat on the trailer hitch. Below the hitch hung an oversized pair of brass balls. *What is it about winter, this town, and pickup trucks?*

"How's the little guy doing?" Nigel eased off the accelerator so there was more distance between the Chev and WIDE ASS.

"He's good. Eating, sleeping, pooping. Being doted upon by everyone in the house."

Nigel smiled. "How come you want to see the Randalls again?

"Something has been nagging at me."

"What's that?" Nigel checked his rear-view mirror.

"Safes."

"What?"

"You know, wall safes. The kind you find in hotel rooms and houses. Safe places for valuables. How come the safe in the Randalls' home wasn't opened? Andrew Pierce buys cars for cash. Cori Pierce buys jewellery in Mexico. It seems it's all about stuff and the money to buy it with. Cash money. The kind of money found in a safe." Lane watched the cloud of exhaust pumping out the back end of WIDE ASS. "Safes are a constant. I checked the reports. In every case there was a safe. And it appeared to be untouched. I want to know if the family remembers what was in their parents' safe. Sometimes a second visit provides significant details, because they've had time to think, or they've noticed something is missing."

"Melissa and David both know they're not suspects, right?" Nigel turned off Crowchild Trail. They passed a mall, then a schoolyard. Nigel turned east, rolled past a park, and stopped in front of a new bungalow on a large lot in a neighbourhood of older houses. Its front drapes were open, and Lane saw Beth stand when she spotted the Chev. She turned to her left, calling out.

As they reached the top step, Beth opened the door. "Come in."

Lane saw she wore a pair of furry black slippers with pink toenails, a red T-shirt, and black sweatpants. "They're in the kitchen." She waited for the detectives to take off their shoes, then led them through the living room and into a kitchen brightened with winter sunlight.

Lane noted the kitchen cabinets were birdseye maple. The taps, fixtures, and marble countertops were all top of the line. He looked at David Randall, who wore a pair of jeans and a blue flannel-lined shirt. Lane stepped forward, shaking hands.

David asked, "Want a cup of coffee?"

"That would be nice." Lane turned to a brown-haired woman who was watching them warily.

"Oh, I forgot you haven't met. This is my wife, Natalie." David stood, moving to the counter. "Cappuccino okay?"

Nigel smiled, nodding in Lane's direction. "You made his day."

"Two?"

Nigel nodded. "Yes, please."

Natalie wore a red top and black jeans. She took one hand away from her coffee cup, tucking a wayward strand of brown hair behind her ear. "Have a seat."

Lane sat down next to Nigel. They heard coffee beans

being ground. Lane watched as David set two cups under the nozzles of a chrome Pasquini espresso machine. Moments later, David set cups down in front of Lane and Nigel, then sat down himself.

David sipped from his mug, waiting.

Lane took a sip. "Very nice. Thank you."

Nigel said, "You aren't suspects. We checked your alibis, and you're all in the clear."

"What about my sister?" David asked.

"Her alibi checks out, too," Lane said. *It'll be interesting to see what happens next.*

"Why are you here, then?" Natalie asked.

Nigel hitched his thumb at Lane. "He wants to ask about the safe."

"Why?" Natalie asked.

Now you're the one being interrogated. For a moment, Lane fought the urge to wrestle back control of the interview. *They aren't suspects. They just want answers.* "I can't tell you everything, but it's an anomaly in this case. Sometimes the answers to anomalies end up being things leading to the killer." Lane turned to David. "What did your parents keep in the safe?"

"That's not the question we have." Natalie pointed at her daughter.

Lane waited. He could hear Nigel inhaling.

"A brooch and necklace are missing. Elizabeth promised them to Beth. She kept them in the safe." Natalie kept her eyes on Lane.

"Either Aunt Peg took them or the killers did," Beth said.

"Dad kept cash in there. It was a habit of his. He always had some on hand. It was gone when I checked. In fact, when you were at the house, I showed you the safe was empty except for a copy of their will. I was so distracted by Peg and everything else. I've only now begun to wonder what happened to the money." David looked out the window at the sun sitting atop the snow-draped evergreens in Confederation Park.

Lane nodded.

Beth wiped at her eyes. "I mentioned it to Donna at Platinum. I said that everyone should keep start-over money. That's what my grandfather called it."

"Was there anyone around who could have overheard?" Lane asked.

"There's always someone listening at a hair salon." Natalie shrugged.

"Did I get them killed?" Beth asked.

Lane shook his head. "No."

Nigel looked at Beth. "You are *not* responsible for what happened. We're after the people who are."

Lane looked at David. "How much would he keep in there?"

"Maybe three hundred thousand in cash and gold. Like Beth said, it was his start-over money."

"There was more, actually." Natalie set her cup down.

Everyone turned to look at her.

"Elizabeth planned to surprise everyone this weekend. It's Beth's birthday. She was going to go to a dealership with Beth and buy a car. Then she would tell Beth she could drive it after she got some lessons. Mom said she always wanted to go into a dealership and buy a car with cash. She'd been planning it for a year."

Lane looked at Beth, who stared at the floor. "Do you have a description of the brooch and the necklace?"

David said, "We have pictures. Dad kept them for insurance." He reached for an iPad.

Lane looked at Nigel, who leaned closer to see the images. The brooch and the necklace were a matched set made of a cluster of green jade stones set in rings of gold.

"Dad had them made for my mother," David said.

"We don't know where they went. They should have been in the safe, but..." Natalie shrugged. "We looked for them yesterday, when we went to the house."

"Would you send us the image, please?" Nigel set down his business card, writing an e-mail address on the back.

David took the card. Then he began tapping the screen of his iPad. "Done."

"There's something else," Natalie leaned forward. "I talked with Linda Sanders. Her parents were killed in Playa del Carmen. She said her mother sent her an e-mail the day before she was murdered. Her mother said she'd run into her hairdresser from home and had plans to meet her and her partner for dinner. She also told me she thought her parents were killed because they had cash and bonds stored in their room safe. They were going to invest in Mexico. Her father didn't trust the banks down there. He thought there was too much corruption."

Lane nodded, looking out the window. *We're close.* "Did the mother mention the hairdresser by name?"

"No, but she went to the same salon as Elizabeth," Natalie said.

Lane stood up, looking at Nigel, who looked back with an intensity Lane hadn't seen before.

"Actually, there's one thing we really need help with. David can't sleep. He wakes at the smallest noise. He's afraid the killers will come after us. Beth is the same." Natalie looked at the detectives with tears brimming.

Nigel said, "You'll be the first to know when we have the killers."

In fifteen minutes the Chev was warming up and they were on their way back downtown. Nigel shifted into low as they started down a hill, preventing them from becoming a curling rock on a patch of black ice. Nigel looked in his rear-view mirror as they passed under the 16th Avenue Bridge, beginning the descent to the Bow River. "This could get real interesting."

Lane heard the engine pick up speed. He turned, looking through a frost-framed gap in the rear window. A small grey car was doing a lazy series of circles behind them as it spun along the centre line of two lanes. "The driver is staring straight ahead. The cars behind him are slowing."

Nigel got to the left side of the lane where the pea-sized gravel from the sanding trucks gathered and traction was better. "Is he catching up?"

"Nope." Lane watched the man's wide eyes as he stared ahead. The car spun. Lane saw the side of the driver's head and a bulbous nose.

"The light is still green."

Lane watched the cars stacked up behind the spinning grey compact. The grey car slid to the bottom of the hill and — where the road widened into three lanes — spun right though the intersection and up onto the sidewalk as if it was what the driver intended. Nigel eased over, flipping on the lights, driving up onto the sidewalk. "Better check whether he's okay."

Lane got out, walking back through ankle-deep snow. He saw the wipers swinging back and forth on the grey car. As he got within five metres, the driver blinked. Lane looked up the road, seeing traffic slowing to a crawl. He approached the passenger window and heard the hum of an electric motor. A wide-eyed man with black hair sat very close to the steering wheel. "Very scary."

Lane nodded. "You okay?"

The man nodded. "Just catching my breath."

✕

"If we're right about Cori and Andrew Pierce, then what's the next move?" Nigel sat at his desk. He opened a file from David Randall and forwarded it, looking across at Lane's computer screen.

Lane tapped his mouse, opened the new file, and pasted the images of the brooch and necklace at the centre of the screen. "First off, we need to keep a close eye on them."

"We need Phelps."

"The shadow?" Lane turned to his partner, smiling. There was a running joke about Phelps. People said even his mother couldn't remember what he looked like. Officers would forget he was in a meeting. Phelps was a master at blending in, often using the talent to disappear when a meeting went too long.

Nigel nodded, smiling. "You all right?"

What's this about? "I'm sorry for what I said about you not being able to save your mom."

What might have been a shrug turned into something like a convulsion. "You were probably right about that. Right now I'm talking about Indiana and worrying about what your sister might do."

Lane looked at the floor. "Christine is tied up in knots. She was doing so well at school. We were all looking forward to the baby. Her life was looking up. Now she won't leave the house for fear of losing Indiana."

"How come she's like that?" Nigel looked sideways at his computer. A message from Anna popped up. *Meet me at eight tonight.*

"My sister or Christine?" Lane looked up from the floor.

"Your sister."

"I don't know." Lane glanced at the door, making sure it was closed.

"What was she like as a kid?" Nigel leaned back in his chair.

Lane looked at the ceiling. "People loved her. She was very good at telling people what they wanted to hear. Most people took her at face value. But there was a nasty side to her. And she was entitled."

"To what?"

"To whatever. She acted like she had a pipeline to God and a ticket to heaven."

"I don't follow the reasoning."

"Neither do I." Lane looked at his screen. "I'll e-mail Phelps."

"Good idea." Nigel shut down his computer, then stood up. "I've got to get going."

What's this all about? Lane saw toilet paper strung across the branches of the mugo pines planted out front of his house. There was a sliver of light visible through a gap in the curtains. He saw eyes and a nose. The light was on at the front door as he went up the steps.

Arthur opened the door. "It happened about an hour ago. Maria next door called. She spotted them. Matt and Dan went out the door, but they got away."

"Who?" Lane closed the door behind him as he unzipped his jacket and took off his toque.

"Three people. A pickup was waiting for them down at the school." Arthur walked into the kitchen. "Christine says it's a trick the kids from Paradise used to play. She thinks they're telling her they can get to Indiana any time they like."

Lane felt the rage starting somewhere just beneath his ribs. He could feel the heat rising to his face and the tips of his ears. "How is Christine handling it?"

Arthur turned, looked at Lane, raised his eyebrows, and leaned his head to the right. "Better than you."

×

Nigel sat down across from Anna where she tapped the screen of an iPad.

"How come you always wear black?" she asked without looking up.

"What do you mean?" Nigel watched Anna through the flat mauve tinted-lenses of her steampunk goggles.

"Black jacket, black pants, black socks, black shoes, black shirt. Need I say more?" Anna continued to tap the screen.

"It's easier."

"Easier than what?" She stopped typing, looking at him.

"Than choosing what to wear every morning. Also, it's easier to blend in."

"Hmmm. Zombies don't blend in." She went back to tapping the iPad screen.

Just wait. She'll get around to it. Nigel closed his eyes, leaning his head back. He shoved his hands into the pockets of his winter jacket.

"I don't think it's over yet with Milton. I recommend we keep going after the money. If Milton's gone to the trouble of hiding that much, it means the money is very important to him. Even now he continues to move it around to keep it safe. The trail is easy to follow. If I keep going after the money, he will eventually understand he needs to stay away from the child or lose his fortune."

Nigel looked up to see Anna was watching him through the red glass. "The baby's mother is like a prisoner now. She's afraid to leave the house because she's sure someone is waiting to take the baby."

Anna blinked. "Do you think she'll be able to handle another week or two?"

"I don't know."

"Milton will be wondering who's behind the transfers. He will eventually come to the conclusion that if he continues to support the abduction of the child, it will continue to cost him. The time factor is the only uncertainty now. Another anonymous donation is in the works." Anna looked at her screen. "Buy some new clothes. Black is depressing and doesn't suit you."

chapter 14

The Calgary Police Service is asking for help from the public. Two high-profile homicides and few leads have led in this appeal.

CUT TO DEPUTY CHIEF CAMERON HARPER, CALGARY POLICE SERVICE "We are asking for the public's help in our investigation of the murders of Elizabeth and Robert Randall, and Megan and Douglas Newsome. A dedicated tips hotline has been set up. It appears at the bottom of your screen. The CPS thanks you in advance for your help in bringing the person or persons responsible for these crimes to justice."

Deputy Chief Harper would not comment when asked if the CPS believes the city faces the threat of a serial killer.

Shazia Wajdan, CBC News, Calgary.

"We get the day shift. Phelps and his partner will take nights." Lane made a sideways glance at Nigel, who wore a purple shirt and sat behind his computer.

"A friend told me I needed more colour." He looked down at the new shirt, flicking away a speck of dust.

"It works for you."

Nigel nodded. "So, what happened?"

This is fucking annoying! It's okay when I'm reading minds, but having mine read is pissing me off. "Toilet paper."

Nigel looked sideways at Lane. "You're going to explain, right?"

"I got home last night and the pine trees at the front of the house were decorated with toilet paper."

"Arthur wouldn't like that."

Lane looked at his computer screen. "Christine says it's a warning. People from Paradise are saying they can get at Indiana anytime they want."

"Toilet paper?"

"Apparently toilet papering someone's property is a prank played by people from her old community."

Nigel's eyebrows met in the middle. "How did Christine react?"

"It's funny. It kind of made her more resolved. Like they'd gone too far. Now there's no way in hell anyone from Paradise will get near Indiana."

Nigel tapped the space bar of his computer. "You can tell her she has nothing to worry about. Things will work out." He turned to face Lane. "It will just take a little time, that's all."

Lane read the certainty in Nigel's eyes and in his voice. *What are you up to?* "What do you mean?" He glanced over at Nigel's screen. VENEER & PLASTIC was written on a green sticky note stuck to the near side of the monitor.

"I'm just saying things like this have a way of working themselves out." He pointed at his computer screen.

"Harper's message is hitting the news. Maybe it will lull Cori and Andrew Pierce into a false sense of security if they believe we have no leads."

Why did you change the subject, Nigel?

×

Cori Pierce sat in the passenger seat of the Porsche Cayenne. Her husband drove as they eased their way along 17th Avenue SW. Western Canada High School, a hodge-podge of connected buildings, was ahead. A white war memorial stood out front of the main building.

"I applied there, but they wouldn't let me in. I've done well for myself despite them." Cori looked sideways at her husband, frowning as he looked side to side for a place to park. "I want to get a pair of shoes before we leave." She pointed at the retro windows of a shoe store.

"Okay." He stopped, putting on his signal light. A car ahead of them was pulling out of a parking space in front of the restaurant.

"What day do I sign the papers for the house?"

"Tuesday." He pulled ahead, shifting into reverse, then turning to look over his shoulder.

"We'll have enough?" Cori began to button up the front of her white winter jacket.

"More than enough. All we're taking with us is the X5." He grimaced when the right rear tire rubbed against the curb.

"Careful. This one's already sold." She caressed the leather seat. "I'm going to miss these heated seats."

"We won't need heated seats anymore." Andrew shifted into drive, easing ahead.

"How about we do a two-fer on Saturday night?"

Andrew looked right at her. "What do you have in mind?"

"Two houses. Two families. Two jobs. A two-fer. Then we get in the car and leave for Cancun."

"Two families? I'll have to get two kits ready, then. Tell me more."

Cori looked at the crowd jammed inside the nearly opaque front door of the restaurant. "Did you make a reservation?"

✕

Lane and Nigel parked a block away from the Pierces' Porsche. Snow and ice stuck to the roof and hood of the detectives' grey mid-sized Ford. Lane watched from the passenger side as Cori and Andrew stepped onto the sidewalk and into a restaurant.

Nigel left the engine running to keep them from freezing to the seats.

A stroller with three large wheels passed on Lane's right. The toddler held a bottle between hands covered with blue mitts. The child was bundled in a snowsuit and blanket. A pair of adults followed. The mother pushed with one hand, sipping steam from a white paper cup. The father followed, took a white cup away from his mouth, smiled, exhaling warm air. There was a relaxed way about them as the stroller bumped over the uneven, snow-cleared sidewalk. The woman leaned into the man, then leaned over to check on the child.

"Don't worry. Your niece and her baby will be fine. I've got a good feeling." Nigel looked left down the length of 17th Avenue. The road rose up to intersect with 4th Street.

Lane turned, studying his partner. "I'm the one who runs on intuition, not you. What the hell is going on?"

Nigel smiled, pointing ahead. "They're getting back into the Porsche. Maybe the restaurant is full."

✕

Lane stepped through the front door of his house, noting the kitchen was filled with family even though it was after eight o'clock. Matt turned right. Lane saw his nephew was holding a plastic bag of ice against a red and swollen left eye and cheek.

Lane kicked off his boots, dropping his winter jacket on the front room easy chair. "What happened?" He moved into the kitchen where Arthur, Matt, and Dan sat. Indiana was sucking eagerly on a bottle. Sam lay on the rug by the door, watching Lane without lifting his chin off the floor.

"Two guys jumped Matt," Arthur said.

"Where are Christine and Alex?" Lane stood at Matt's shoulder.

"They went shopping. Matt took the dogs out for a walk." Dan spoke quietly. Indiana released the bottle. There was a sound of hissing air. His eyes closed, opened, then he resumed eating.

Something is missing, Lane thought. "You okay?" Lane looked down at Matt.

"I'm fine. Just got punched once. Then Roz went after the guy. Sam thought it was a game and jumped in as well. I took out the second guy's knee just like you taught me. Then this lady in an SUV drove up. She started honking her horn. There was a baby in the back seat of the vehicle. The one guy helped the other into a pickup. He shouted they'd be back with more guys to take care of me. Then they drove away. The lady in the SUV — she said she knew you — helped me put Roz in the back of her truck, then drove us to the vet's."

Lane looked around and under the table. "Where's Roz?"

Arthur said, "Roz is dead. One of the guys kicked her. The vet says it broke a couple of ribs. A bone fragment penetrated her heart."

Lane felt his shoulders drop. Matt stood up, got his uncle a chair, waited for him to sit down. "When did this happen?" Lane asked.

Arthur said, "A little over two hours ago."

Matt pulled the ice away from his eye. "I don't know what else I could have done."

Sam rubbed up against Arthur, who scratched the dog behind the ears. "The woman who helped Matt, her name is Donna. She got the licence plate of the attacker's pickup. She drove Matt to the vet's and then home. I called it in. The officer took the information and said he'd call back. I left a message with Erinn. About twenty minutes after that, Harper phoned, asking what happened. He said he would call back."

Lane looked at Indiana, now snoring in Dan's arms. The baby had a smile on his face.

chapter 15

Accused's Donation Clouds Legal Process

Efram Milton of Paradise, Alberta, has made a major gift to the Alberta Children's Hospital's Neo-natal Intensive Care Unit in Calgary.

Rhonda Kruden, spokesperson for the Alberta Children's Hospital, confirmed the contribution. "Last Friday, a donation in the amount of one million dollars was made in the name of Mr. Milton. Needless to say, we're thrilled."

Crown Counsel Robert Wilson was asked how Milton could afford a donation of one million dollars when has he previously requested legal aid.

At a court appearance in January, Milton testified that he was unable to afford legal representation. Wilson says,

"If the report on the donation is confirmed, then Mr. Milton will also be charged with perjury."

Milton's current attorney, Joseph Lane, says, "Mr. Milton made a substantial contribution to a worthy charity. He deserves praise for his generosity, not threats of prosecution."

But Milton's actions may not be so clear-cut, says Mount Royal University law professor Lyle McDougal. "If this is an attempt by Milton to garner public support for his fight to protect his 'religious freedom', after his alleged involvement in an attempted child abduction, the tactic appears to have backfired."

Lori poked her head into Lane's office. "Harper and Simpson want to see you as soon as possible."

"Me?" Lane pointed at his chest.

"Both of you." Lori pointed at them with the first two fingers of her right hand.

Ten minutes later, they waited outside of the Chief's office where his secretary tapped at a keyboard and answered the phone.

Chief Simpson's door opened, and he poked his head out the door. "Sorry to keep you waiting. Come in."

Nigel followed Lane inside where Deputy Chief Cam Harper sat in one of four chairs set around the coffee table. Dwarfing everyone else in the room, Harper stood to shake hands with the detectives. He had apparently surrendered to the inevitability of an ever-expanding bald patch by shaving his head.

All sat down and Simpson started the meeting. "We've been gathering information on the assault involving your nephew."

This isn't what I expected. "What have you found out, exactly?"

Harper glanced at a sheet of paper on the coffee table. "Two men were taken into custody last night at the Rockyview Hospital. One had injuries to his knee. The other had dog bites to both legs."

There was a knock at the door. Harper rose, returning with a tray of four cups of coffee, sugar, and cream.

Nigel leaned forward, grabbing a cup.

"What are their names?" Lane asked.

"Robert Pratt and Michael Milton, both of Paradise. Their story is they were assaulted by a man with two dogs." Harper reached for his coffee.

Simpson sat back.

Lane looked out the window at the white smoke rising

from the heating-plant chimney across the street. The sky behind the smoke was winter blue.

Simpson said, "An independent witness named Donna Laughton made a report indicating Pratt and Milton pulled up in a truck, exited the vehicle, and proceeded to assault Matt."

"It matches with what Matt told me last night." Lane looked at the coffee, decided to wait.

"Is Matt okay?" Harper asked.

Lane nodded. "Black eye. Tommy Pham called last night and wants pictures. He wants evidence because he thinks the assault and the attempted abduction are connected. And now it appears that's what you are saying."

Simpson nodded. "It looks like it. Pratt and Milton have been tightlipped, but we have established they are well connected in Paradise."

Harper crossed his right leg over his left. "We want to know how you and your family are doing."

Lane shrugged. "It's tough. Christine finally got out last night and then this happened. She was pretty upset when she got home. At least now she's wanting to fight back instead of hiding out."

"And Arthur?" Harper asked.

"Looking after everyone else." Lane gave in and leaned forward, adding sugar and milk to his coffee. He sat back and sipped.

"Dan and the baby?" Simpson asked.

"Seem to be okay. Dan's kind of hunkered down. Indy is oblivious and pretty content." Lane wrapped his fingers around the cup. "In fact, Indy keeps us laughing."

"There have been related developments." Simpson nodded at Harper.

"At least two sizable withdrawals have been made from Milton's bank accounts. One was the donation to the

Children's Hospital. People who regularly contribute to the Red Cross made a series of donations that total up to the other. A sample was contacted. None could recall making the donations. Milton's lawyer has some questions about the transfers." Harper studied Lane, then Nigel.

Lane said, "That's odd. I've been wondering about that as well. Especially since the donations indicate Milton perjured himself when he requested legal assistance. He claimed he didn't have the financial resources to fight a polygamy trial." He looked back at Harper and then at Simpson.

"What about the Randall investigation?" Harper asked.

Nigel said, "We are tracking two persons of interest."

"Cori and Andrew Pierce?" Simpson asked.

Nigel nodded. "That's correct."

Harper leaned forward. "So it's clear Byron Thomas is in jail for a crime he didn't commit?"

Lane put his cup down. "We're both convinced Thomas is innocent. At this point, our focus is to prevent any further murders and gather sufficient evidence to arrest those responsible. We have added another team to follow the Pierces."

Nigel said, "We also discovered they've recently added a second mortgage to their house, effectively removing equity from their home. Border authorities have been alerted to their status and their identities."

"So do we have them on false identities?" Simpson asked.

Nigel shrugged. "Probably."

Harper glanced at Simpson before saying, "We need as many teams as possible to track the suspects without jeopardizing the investigation. The first priority is to prevent further killings. The second is to arrest the actual killers this time. There will inevitably be fallout, because the wrong man was arrested and other murders have occurred as a result. We need to deal with that. You two need to get the killers off the street."

Lane looked at the Chief and Harper in turn.

Simpson asked, "Phelps is on this?"

"Night shift," Lane said.

"All of the other murders took place at night?" Harper asked.

"That's correct." Lane waited, then asked, "What about Roz?"

"What?" Harper asked.

Simpson studied Lane.

"Either Pratt or Milton killed my dog," Lane said.

Simpson said, "Your home is covered. There will be no more threats."

Lane stood. "If that's all, we need to get back to work."

Nigel remained quiet for the next few minutes as they made their way back downstairs, then sat at their desks. Lane waited.

"They killed your dog? How come you didn't tell us?"

Lane looked at the wall. "I just got in when we were called to go upstairs. You can imagine how my family reacted. Even Sam, the other dog, is in shock. By the way, you didn't have much to say at the meeting. Not like you at all."

"Don't change the subject. You nailed me with the comment about how I'm punishing myself for not being able to save my mother. So answer my question."

Lane looked at Nigel's face, seeing the resolve and a bit of a smile at the corners of his mouth. "It's hard to talk about Roz. She was part of the family. My family is threatened, and I feel like there isn't much I can do to help them."

"Was that so difficult?"

Lane tried to smile. "Yes."

It was a couple of hours later, while they were waiting outside of Platinum Hair Salon, that Lane wondered, *Why did Nigel change the subject when I asked him why he was so quiet in the meeting?*

×

The streetlight cast a soft glow on the pavement where Lane walked next to Matt. Sam pulled on the leash when he spotted a dog across the street.

"No!" Matt growled.

Lane used his right hand to grab hold of Sam's leash. They walked on a patch of pathway that hadn't been shovelled. The snow was compacted into a slippery crust, making footing precarious.

The dog across the street passed. Sam tried to turn but found himself caught between two humans who were ready for him. He reared up on his hind legs, whimpering, then surrendered to walking between Matt and Lane.

"He's a handful." Lane exhaled. His breath formed a cloud in the minus-fifteen-degree air.

"You didn't have to come, you know. I can take care of myself."

Lane looked right at the dark shadow of the bruise just visible between Matt's toque and the turned-up collar of his winter jacket. "I needed a walk."

"You're missing Roz too?"

"Yep. She had attitude. I liked that in her." He smiled.

Matt chuckled. "A lot like Christine and Alex."

"Exactly."

"I'm glad Christine went out last night. She needs to do that more often." Matt turned right at the corner. Sam and Lane followed. They walked in the snow along the side of the road where traction was better.

Lane's phone rang. He reached into his pocket, didn't recognize the phone number, frowned, pressed the answer button, and put the phone to his ear. "Hello."

"Paul, is that you?"

"That's right."

"What the hell do you think you're doing?"

Lane looked at Matt, who stopped to listen to the conversation. "Who is this?"

"Joseph. Your brother! Don't you recognize my voice?"

Obviously not. "What do you want?"

"I don't know how you did it, but it has to stop now!"

"You're talking about the court case?" Lane looked at the stars. *In all of the infinity of possibilities, how did I get stuck with you and Alison for siblings?*

"You know damned well I'm not talking about the court case. I'm talking about the money!"

"Whose money?" Lane held the phone several centimetres from his ear.

"My money! Milton's money!"

Lane looked at Matt, who rolled his eyes. "I have no idea what you're talking about."

"Money from my account and Milton's account has been donated to the Children's Hospital and the Red Cross."

Don't say it. Don't say it. "That's very kind of the two of you." *Shit, you went right ahead and said it.*

"Listen to me, you fucking Pauline! Stay away from our money. In particular, stay away from my money!"

"I'll say this one more time. I don't know what you are talking about. And tell Milton and Alison to stay away from my family!" Lane looked at his phone.

"She has a right..."

Lane pressed *end*, then shut off the power to the phone.

"What was that all about?" Matt stood with his arms crossed. Sam sat looking up with a quizzical expression.

"Joseph is upset."

"Thanks, Captain Obvious. What's really going on?"

"Apparently someone has been getting into Joseph and Milton's accounts and donating their money to charities. Joseph thinks I'm responsible."

"Are you?"

"No." Lane took a step. Sam followed.

Matt held the leash. "You know who is responsible, don't you?"

Lane stopped and turned. "I think so." Sam looked from one to the next.

"Who is it?"

"I don't want to say until I'm sure."

"And you've got a killer to catch."

Lane nodded. "That too."

chapter 16

Calgary Lawyer Donates to Red Cross

The Red Cross has received a belated Christmas gift by way of a million-dollar donation from Calgary lawyer Joseph Lane.

Red Cross spokesperson Mary Latourneau says, "This gift and other recent donations will go a long way toward helping us provide for refugees around the globe. I would like to thank Mr. Joseph Lane for his very generous donation." The role of philanthropist is new to Lane, and he wears it well.

When contacted about his extraordinary generosity, Lane said, "The Red Cross does admirable work all over the world. My family has done very well by working and living in Calgary. It's time for us to give back."

Letourneau says, "January and February are often slow months for us. This year we have been overwhelmed by the generosity of Albertans."

"Have you got both kits together for Saturday night?" Cori sipped a cappuccino. The morning light reflected off the white cupboards and the white arabescato corchia marble countertop in their kitchen. She tucked in the top of her white robe.

"I'll do that tonight. First I need to pick up some new gloves and booties. I did check the ammunition. We've got plenty. I'll be able to pick up some more on the drive south." Andrew wore his grey Meyer pants and blue tailor-made shirt. He fiddled with the stainless-steel cappuccino machine. "Are the passports ready?" He stepped sideways, opening the fridge door. The milk carton was in the door above two plastic blood bags. He grabbed the milk, closing the door with his foot.

Cori nodded. "I've got to get an outfit for Saturday's party, especially those shoes. Then I'm off to work."

"Another protégé to instruct?" Andrew turned, smiling at her.

Her eyes sparkled as she set her cup down. "If the opportunity presents itself."

"Want me to leave a cheque for Roza?"

Cori shook her head, winking. "Payday isn't until next Monday. We get free maid service this month."

Lane and Nigel parked down the street from the Pierce home. Nestled under the limbs of a spruce tree, they had a clear view of the two-storey infill with its river rock front, copper pillars, peaked roofs, and oval windows. The combined effect gave the impression that the home was afloat on a white prairie sea.

"You enjoying going back to school?" Nigel worked the heat dials of the white Jeep as he sat in the passenger seat. It appeared impossible to find a comfortable temperature. He unzipped his jacket, then rolled down the window.

"To tell you the truth, it's been fascinating. The guy's teaching about the psychology of bullying, then exhibits the same aggressive behaviours he describes in his lectures. And he appears to be totally unaware of the contradiction." Lane saw the light come on at the front of the three-car garage.

"Sounds like my dad. He saw himself as being fair minded and logical. His behaviour was the opposite." Nigel zipped up his coat.

Now's the time to ask. "I got an interesting call last night while Matt and I were walking the dog."

Nigel took his gloves off. "Oh?"

"My brother phoned to ask why I was messing around with his and Efram Milton's money."

Nigel pulled on his toque. "You're kidding."

There was a slight intake of breath before he answered and a bit of a quiver in his voice. "He was pretty agitated."

"Money often gets people motivated."

"I said I didn't know what he was talking about." Lane watched as the garage door opened.

"Keep in touch." Nigel climbed out, shut the door, and walked back to a nondescript Chevy SUV.

Your non-answers are answers, Nigel.

Lane looked through the glass at the wood fire. A chef in a white coat hefted a wooden paddle, slipping it under a pizza inside the oven, removing it, and sliding it onto a plate. Then he used the paddle to check under a second pizza. The detective's eyes moved to take in the poster-sized black-and-white photographs on the walls. People were frozen in the day-to-day activities of Naples. In one, a man kissed a woman on the cheek. Her eyes were not amused.

"Lane? How was work today?" Lane turned to face Dan, who sat on the white bench holding a sleeping Indiana.

You look tired. "I spent the day sitting for the most part." *Surveillance is tedious in the extreme.*

"Here, let me hold him." Alex sat between Lane and Matt. She had insisted they all go out for supper.

Dan looked at Christine, who nodded. He lifted the baby over the table. Arthur put his hand underneath just in case. Alex tucked Indiana in the crook of her left elbow, caressing his cheek with her knuckles.

The waiter escorted a couple to a nearby table. The couple glanced, smiling at the baby. Five pairs of adult eyes assaulted them. Their friendly smiles straight-lined and the couple looked away.

Alex asked, "Can we relax? You told me this was the best pizza place in town. How about we just enjoy a night out? And Matt, your black eye is scaring people."

Dan smiled. "It does look remarkably sinister."

Christine laughed. "Matt will scare the monsters away from Indy's closet."

Two waiters dressed in white shirts and black pants arrived with pizzas. "Quattro stagioni?" Dan raised his hand. The thin-crust pizza was placed before him. He inhaled, rolling his eyes with pleasure.

"Romana?"

"Please." Lane pointed at the place setting in front of him.

"What are those things?" Alex nodded at Lane's pizza.

"Anchovies." He cut a pie-shaped slice, waiting for the inevitable response.

"What?" Alex grimaced.

"Tiny stinky fishies." Christine shook her head.

A second round of pizzas arrived, followed by Matt's calzone. He got busy cutting up Alex's pizza for her.

Alex looked at the dark-haired waiter. "What does *pulcinella* mean?"

The waiter smiled as if he'd been waiting for someone to ask. "A funny guy who makes people laugh."

Indiana smiled. Alex looked down at him, pointing. "He's our funny guy. I've already written about him on my blog."

Lane had been inhaling the scent of tomato sauce, oregano, and basil. He suddenly looked up, eyes wide. He stared blankly at the waiter, who asked, "Is there a problem with the pizza, sir?"

"No, he's just had an epiphany. Or an orgasm. Sometimes it's hard to tell with him." Arthur rolled up a wedge of pizza and closed his eyes, chewing then covering his mouth with his open left hand. "Thank you, Alex! This was a wonderful idea."

The waiter's eyebrows met in the middle; then he rushed away.

chapter 17

This is Shazia Wajdan.

A daring daytime escape occurred on Crowchild Trail this morning. Eyewitness Wayne Long describes what happened.

CUT TO WAYNE LONG "I was following the sheriff's paddy wagon. Two pickup trucks cut me off, then forced the paddy wagon to the side of the road. Guys jumped out of the trucks with long guns. I called 911."

Another eyewitness, who declined to appear on camera, said one of the guards and a prisoner got into one of the pickups and were driven away. The guard in the driver's seat was taken to hospital with undetermined injuries. So far there is no word on the identity of the escaped prisoner.

Shazia Wajdan, CBC News, Calgary.

Lane set the phone in its cradle, turning to a waiting Nigel. "Efram Milton escaped."

Nigel leaned away from his computer. "How?"

"Milton was being transported. The transport van was forced off the road by two pickup trucks. Milton and one of the guards are missing. The other guard is in hospital suffering from a concussion."

Nigel looked at the ceiling. "The missing guard was in on it?"

Lane shrugged. "It's a possibility."

Lane followed Dr. Pierce along one of the walkways connecting the education building to the library tower. A machine with a rolling blue brush threw a cloud of white into the air as it spun snow from the walkway. Pierce was bareheaded, wearing a calf-length cashmere overcoat, a blue scarf, and black leather gloves.

Dr. Pierce turned left, opening one of the heavy glass doors leading into the library foyer. Lane watched as Pierce opened his coat, turning away from the escalator. He walked through a door on the south side of the library.

Lane opened the door, feeling the rush of warm air, but kept his toque on as he followed. Through the open door he saw a room filled with computers. Pierce sat down at a computer with his back to the wall.

Lane backed out of the door, moving to the far side of the escalator to wait. He unzipped his jacket and took off his gloves.

Twenty minutes later, Lane was scratching his head while checking the time on his phone. *This toque is so damned itchy!*

Dr. Pierce appeared in the doorway, buttoning his coat and arranging his scarf.

Lane turned, watching Pierce's reflection in the glass. He waited for the professor to walk outside, then followed him to the parking lot south of the education building where his Porsche was parked. The detective made his way to the Jeep, two rows over with a clear view of the Porsche. Lane climbed into the Jeep, pushed in the clutch, and started the engine. *I wish this thing had heated seats.* He turned on the windshield defroster, then grabbed the gearshift.

Pierce drove toward the south exit facing Father David Bower Arena, turning toward Crowchild Trail. Lane followed the Porsche when it was momentarily out of sight behind a stand of evergreens. Pierce turned onto southbound Crowchild. Lane kept a white pickup between him and the Porsche as they followed Crowchild Trail's descent into the Bow River Valley. When they stopped at a red light, Lane picked up his phone and dialed Lori.

"Yes, Paul?"

"Can you and Nebal check the social media accounts of Cori and Andrew Pierce for any recent entries?"

"Will do." Lori hung up.

The light turned green. Pierce turned left, heading toward Kensington.

Pierce parked in front of the Plaza Theatre. It was a white building built in 1935, nestled between a newer building housing a pair of restaurants and the open face of Pages Bookstore.

We're getting back to where we started. Lane turned down a side street, parking out of sight of Pierce, who walked to the front door of the theater. The billboard above the door announced that *The Big Sleep* was playing. The detective's phone rang. "Lane."

"Nigel. Cori Pierce just parked across from the street from you."

Lane checked his rear-view mirror, seeing her getting out of a grey BMW X5. She wore an ankle-length silver fox fur coat. The collar was tucked up over her ears.

"Got her. Thanks." Lane undid his seat belt.

"I'm down the street to the west."

"The professor went to the Plaza. That's probably where she's headed."

"I've got a good spot here to watch the front door. You want to take the back?"

Lane recognized the smile in Nigel's voice. "You've got a nice warm spot?"

"Gotta love these heated seats. The suspects are out in front of the theatre. Keep close to the storefronts, then duck into the bookstore. But first, look up." Nigel hung up.

What the hell does that mean? Lane didn't see Cori Pierce near the front of the Plaza. He climbed out of the Jeep, locking it. Then he pulled on his toque, stepping over a pile of crusty snow left by a plow, and walked across the street, making for Pages Books. *If memory serves, they have a fire escape looking down over the rear of the Plaza.* He opened the front door of the bookstore, spotting several patrons lined up at the counter. He caught a whiff of cigarette smoke and nodded at Sarah. He glanced at the stairs. She smiled. Lane climbed the stairs, unzipping his coat and taking off his toque and mitts. The wall was adorned with black-and-white photographs of writers in literary poses.

He got to the top of the stairs, turned right, and looked out the rear window. A spider's web of power lines crisscrossed the alleyway. Lane used his right hand to push back a curtain and open a metal door. He stepped out onto the staircase and closed the door behind him. A woman wearing a tan wool coat stood halfway down the fire escape. Looking out over the cars parked below, she brought a cigarette to her lips. Simone glanced over her shoulder, taking another hit of nicotine and nodding at the detective. "Come out to enjoy the sky?" She tipped her head to the right.

Lane looked at the belly of a smoky-blue chinook, then to the west, where the edge of the arch met blue sky. *That's what Nigel was talking about!*

"Can you feel it warming up?" Simone tapped the filter tip of her cigarette on the railing.

The wind was shifting, coming from the west. He felt its warm hand on his face. He smiled. "I was wondering if I could borrow your staircase."

Simone looked to her left as if listening to a conversation. She put her forefinger to her lips, signalling him to join her.

Lane tiptoed down the stairs. Simone pointed between the buildings. A foot-wide gap separated the cinderbrick wall of the bookstore and the brick wall of the theatre. At the far end of the narrow opening stood several metres of wall. Voices carried over the wall, along the gap between the buildings, to their ears.

Lane leaned closer to the Plaza Theatre's white wall.

"We're set for Saturday night, then?"

It's a woman's voice.

"I think everything is ready."

That's Andrew Pierce's voice.

"I've got the passports ready," the woman said.

"Still want to do the two-fer?" Pierce asked.

"More than ever. It should launch us internationally. Then we do a D.B. Cooper."

"What's our weekend total?"

"Five."

"I'll need some extra FlexiCuffs," Pierce observed.

"Get them after the show. I'm finished my smoke. Let's go in."

Simone stepped away from the wall. "That's the woman who wanted the books on Olson, Williams, and Homolka.

I saw her coming down the street. Did you hear something you can use?" Simone asked.

"Unfortunately, their conversation would be easy to explain away." Lane looked at the belly of the chinook. *Pierce is getting extra FlexiCuffs. They're planning for two scenes this time.*

×

Lori pointed at her computer screen. "This is kind of weird. Mostly it's arrogant, but it is weird."

Lane went around the counter. There was a photo of Cori Pierce leaning against the hood of an Alpha Romeo. Lori's red fingernail pointed to a post near the top of the social media page.

> Cori and I are frightened by the recent spate of murders in this city. Close acquaintances of ours have been killed. I'm convinced this is the work of a serial killer. The police appear totally inept in their handling of these cases. Cori has told me many of her customers — this city's movers and shakers — are in fear of their lives. How many more of these tragedies will occur before the police finally arrest those responsible?

"When was this posted?" Lane asked.

"About half past two this afternoon." Lori pointed at the screen.

"Was it posted from the U of C?" *The time fits with when Dr. Pierce was in the library.*

"Want me to see what else Nebal can find out?"

"Yes, please," Lane said.

chapter 18

Psychiatric Evaluation Ordered for Accused Child Abductor

A judge has granted an application for a psychiatric assessment for Alison Milton. Joseph Lane, Ms. Milton's lawyer, made the request in court yesterday.

Lane said, "My client has been the victim of relentless abuse. Her polygamist husband Efram Milton's recent escape from custody is evidence of his total disregard for the law and accountability."

During the application, Alison Milton testified, "God told me to take the boy from my daughter and bring him to a place where he will be raised by true believers." In a rambling five-minute speech she also said, "God spoke to me on more than one occasion, telling me the child should be taken to the desert for forty days and forty nights."

Efram Milton of Paradise, Alberta, initially charged as accomplice in the child abduction, escaped custody yesterday and is being sought by police.

"What's the plan for Saturday?" Nigel asked.

Lane looked over at his partner wearing a pink shirt. *There must be a woman behind this colourful change.* "We meet with the team in ten minutes."

Nine minutes later, the conference room was full. Lane looked around the table. Harper sat at the head in his deputy chief uniform. Lori sat next to him with her laptop ready. Grey-haired and square-jawed McTavish wore his grey-blue tactical unit jumpsuit. Nigel was dwarfed sitting beside McTavish. Next to Lane was a nondescript man wearing a grey shirt and pants. His face was round, his eyes and hair were brown, his height and weight were average. Lane recognized him because he was so unremarkable he could be only one person. "Darren? Do you know everyone here?"

Darren Phelps nodded, smiling.

Lane saw Netsky hovering outside the glass door. *Maybe I should invite him in? No way. This has to remain in this room. Netsky was one of Smoke's good ol' boys. He'll repeat whatever he hears, perhaps even leak it to the media.* "This time, we may be a step ahead of our killers. We have a location, and indications are another homicide is planned for Saturday night."

Lori nodded at Lane. "Nebal is tracking the suspects' social media sites, providing regular updates."

"The evidence we've gathered so far is circumstantial, but the threat is a serious one. Each of you will have a specific task on Saturday." Lane nodded at Harper.

Harper leaned forward, looking at Phelps. "We need someone on the inside. Phelps, you'll be working with the caterer serving food. You'll stay behind inside the residence after everyone else leaves."

Harper pointed at McTavish. "You will be stationed nearby in case the tactical unit is required. Pay close attention to weather reports, because the forecast shows a cold front heading our way."

Lane caught Harper's eye, lifting his chin in Lori's direction. Harper nodded. "Lori will be working overtime on the weekend. She'll be monitoring communications and handling any updates. She will centralize, providing backup in case anything goes wrong out on the street."

Lane said, "Nigel and I will be tracking the movements of our suspects. We believe the pair is responsible for as many as twelve murders. Some of the homicides occurred in Calgary. Others occurred in New York, Toronto, and Playa del Carmen. Indications are there may be five murders planned for this weekend."

Lori pointed at her computer. "Pierce has posted another comment on social media. He says the police are looking for the public's help in finding the serial killers responsible for the Randall and Newsome murders because we have no idea who the killers are. He says he and his wife fear for their lives."

Lane said, "There are also indications the pair plans to leave the country early Sunday."

Lane nodded at Nigel, who stood to pass out photographs of Cori and Andrew Pierce. "These are our suspects. Their identities and aliases are at the bottom."

"Any information on the type of weapons they use?" McTavish held up his copies of the pictures of the suspects.

"Fibre's review of three crime scenes shows that a nine-millimetre handgun was used in at least four of the homicides. He also believes they use a box cutter." Lane put his hand on the file in front of him. "You all know your jobs. We keep Lori and the deputy chief informed of any developments. They will make sure that information is passed on to all of us."

Harper stood up. "As always the priority is to protect the public. We need this pair in jail, and we need the evidence to keep them there."

Lane watched the room empty. He looked through the open door and spotted a man in a tailored grey coat talking to Lori. Lane could see only the man's back. *There's something familiar there.* He sensed confrontation in the man's posture.

Lori looked around the man, made eye contact with Lane, and leaned her head to the left.

Lane gathered up his folders and walked out the door. The man in the grey coat turned.

Lane said, "Hello, Joseph."

Joseph didn't offer his hand. "We need to talk."

Lane opened his right hand to direct his brother into his office.

Nigel asked, "Anyone want a coffee?"

Out of his left eye, Lane saw Lori take Nigel to one side. Joseph stepped into Lane's office. The detective followed, closing the door behind him and standing across from his brother, whose silver hair glistened under the fluorescent lights. Lane waited. *Have you got some new hair, Joseph, or is that a wig?*

"This has to stop now," Joseph said.

"I agree. Christine deserves to be free to raise her son without fear." Lane stood in front of the door with his arms crossed, his feet apart.

"I'm not talking about Christine." Joseph undid the top two buttons of his coat to reveal a white shirt, a red tie, and a navy-blue pinstriped suit.

Then what are you talking about? Lane decided to wait.

"Maybe you think you have a right to do what you're doing, but that money is my retirement savings. And yes, I'm defending Alison because she's my sister. She's your sister, too. Yes, she believes she speaks to God, and she has an unusual lifestyle, but she is our sister." Joseph undid two more buttons. "It's hot in here."

Lane felt a tremor in his hand. He looked down and saw his right hand shaking. "Start at the beginning." He sat down at his desk. Joseph took off his coat, folded it over his right arm, and sat in Nigel's chair.

"I have to defend her. She asked me to. I couldn't say no."

"How would you feel if she tried to abduct your child or grandchild, then transport the baby to the States where it could disappear into a polygamist compound?"

Joseph looked back at his brother. His eyes narrowed. "You know this for certain?"

Lane nodded. "Sarah told it to the arresting officers when they interviewed her."

"They were taking Indiana to the States?"

Lane nodded.

"Efram said that Alison just wanted the baby —" Joseph looked sideways at Lane "— to have a good home."

"That's what Christine wants, and she's Indiana's mother. She's also the person who escaped Paradise because she saw her name on the bishop's fuck chart." Lane studied his brother's reaction.

Joseph leaned back in his chair then took a breath. "Christine told you that?"

"That's right. The excommunication happened after she left. She escaped Paradise and came to you, remember?" *It still hurts to know Christine went to you first. And it still galls me that you turned her away, Joseph.*

"Margaret said she couldn't stay. I wasn't there."

And your wife must have said it was okay to defend Alison against Christine or we wouldn't be here. "Christine, her child, and the child's father deserve the right to live free from fear."

"And I want you to stop donating my money to charity."

"I know nothing about that."

Joseph stared back at his brother. "You must have an idea."

Lane stared back at his brother. "Can you guarantee that Christine, Dan, and Indy will be left alone?"

"Okay. If that's what it takes, you have my guarantee. I will make sure Alison will leave them alone. Milton has other things to worry about now, and the word is our sister's being excommunicated." Joseph stood and began to put on his coat. "The judge agreed to my request for a psychiatric evaluation for our sister. I think the doctor's report will strengthen her case." He walked to the door, putting his hand on the door handle. "Consider this information an act of good faith. I will hold you personally responsible if more of my assets go missing." Joseph took his time buttoning his coat, opening the door, and stepping out.

Lane turned to his computer, tapping the mouse. His map of the murder suspects stared back at him, but he didn't see it.

"Here's your coffee." Nigel set a mug down in front of his partner, then sat at his desk. "Who was that?"

"My brother." Lane sensed the stillness in Nigel, the expectation. "Two things."

Nigel sipped his coffee, watching Lane.

"Our first priority is to prevent the Pierces from hurting anyone else."

Nigel nodded.

"The second is whoever is transferring money out of my brother's accounts is going to stop." Lane looked at Nigel. "Understood?"

Nigel took another sip before nodding.

✕

Nigel found Anna in her library chair. She had on a pair of black pants and high faux-leather boots. Her blonde hair was red tipped, a shade darker than her red sweater. She flipped up the lenses of her glasses to watch his approach.

He sat down across from her. "I'm glad you wore pink." She pointed at his shirt.

"I took your suggestion about wearing more colour."

"The library closes at nine."

Nigel reached into his pocket, lifted out his phone, and glanced at the time. "We've got ten minutes."

"Okay." She reached for her iPad, set it on her lap, and crossed her legs.

"Can you back off on the lawyer?"

Anna shrugged. "No problem. Can I still go after Milton and the Pierces?"

Nigel nodded, then asked, "What did you find out about the Pierces?"

"He's writing stuff on social media sites. She's withdrawing money from several accounts."

Nigel nodded. "You're sure it's him?"

"Of course. I hacked his personal computer. Then I went into his encrypted files where he keeps some original documents." She handed him her iPad. "Take a look at what I found. He's planning some blogs. He uses a phony e-mail account to send them back and forth so he can deny they're his."

Studying Your Prey

The Murderer's Lifestyle

Hiding in Plain Sight

Knowing When to Stop

Creating a New Identity

Cash Is King for a Killer

Creating a Diversion

Physical Fitness Regime

Smuggling Weapons Across the Border

Living Off Investments

Nigel handed the iPad back, looking at her for a moment. *I can't use this information as evidence.* "Those two are very dangerous."

Anna said, "He and his wife are total narcissists."

"They might come after you." Nigel felt a wave of dread wash over him.

"They have no idea I'm accessing their personal information."

"Can you wait until Sunday to go after their money?"

Anna nodded. Her entire upper body emphasized the affirmation. She smiled. "I have a plan."

×

Christine and Indiana were waiting in the living room for Lane when he walked in the front door just after ten o'clock. He could hear Indiana sucking and sighing as he fed at Christine's breast. She had a blanket overtop the baby's head. Indiana had his ankles crossed. Lane asked, "Where is everyone?"

"Asleep." She looked at her son. "He's done nothing but eat and poop all day long." Indiana farted and sighed, as if to point out he didn't want to be left out of the conversation.

Lane smiled, took off his coat, hung it up, and kicked off his boots, feeling the fatigue loosen its grip when he saw the smile on Christine's face.

"Sylvia phoned." Christine adjusted her breast under the blanket.

You're a natural with that baby. "Tommy Pham's wife?"

"She calls herself his assistant. She's very nice. She said my mom is going to undergo a psychiatric examination."

"I heard that too."

"From who?"

"My brother."

"Joseph came to see you?"

Lane heard disbelief in her voice. "Surprised me too."

"Do you think this means my mom is crazy?"

"Mental illness would certainly explain some of her behaviour. I'm just not sure what it will mean in the long run."

"Could it be a step in the right direction, though?"

Lane nodded. "It looks like Alison is excommunicated, and Milton is on the run."

"This is a good thing?"

"I hope so. The problem is I've learned not to trust my brother or my sister."

"Me too." Christine smiled as Indiana wrapped a hand around her forefinger.

chapter 19

"Donna Liu called. She asked you to meet her at this address at eleven o'clock." Lori leaned to one side of her computer so she could see him and held up a piece of paper.

Lane stopped, backtracked, picked up the piece of paper, and read the address. "It's her house."

"She said she'd be there at that time. Something about waiting for contactors, taking her son to the doctor, and going to the bank. It sounded like she was in a rush."

Lane stepped into his office, spotted Nigel behind his computer. "Grab your coat. We gotta go."

Five minutes later they drove past the Bow Tower, a blue glass building shaped like a wave with crisscrossing metal beams reaching over two hundred metres. It appeared to be tickling the belly of the chinook arch. The warm winds had turned snow, ice, sand, and salt into a kind of brown soup coating city roads and sidewalks.

"I need to let you know about a few things." Nigel concentrated on the traffic, anticipating the movements of an SUV crabbing across three lanes of traffic. It hit a patch of brown snow. A brown wave of the soupy mixture hit their windshield. Nigel turned on the wipers.

Lane looked left at his partner. "All right."

"I've know Anna for years. She was always kind of out there. We knew she was smart. She used to drive her parents and the teachers crazy, because she would never hand in any assignments. I asked her about it one time, and she told me handing stuff in for marks was against her ethics. Then she got into trouble because she thought a teacher was unfair to one of the kids in her class. Anna hacked into the system's computers and changed the kid's mark. One of the other kids found out and told someone. They caught Anna, and she was suspended for a week. She was our hero from then on. I went to her after my dad killed my mom, because I knew he'd hidden money away in various accounts. I didn't want to live with my uncle and aunt, and I needed money. Anna agreed to get the money for me. We worked out a business arrangement. She got a percentage, and I got enough money to keep me going for at least fifteen years. After we graduated, we kept in touch."

Lane looked down along 6th Avenue. "How did she graduate if she never handed anything in?"

Nigel smiled. "At the time, provincial exams counted for fifty percent of our grade twelve marks. She got one-hundred percent on every one of her exams."

"She went to university?"

Nigel shook his head. "She went freelance. She tracks down information about various political and financial institutions. She calls it massaging investments. Prides herself with getting in and out without anyone being the wiser. Again, it's all guided by her ethics."

"What does that mean?"

"Let's just say if the people who were screwed by Bernie Madoff and other Ponzi schemes hired her, they would be smiling today."

"How smart is she?" Lane opened his jacket to cool off. He looked left, spotting a guy wearing shorts and a hoodie walking along the river pathway with a package in his arms.

"I don't know the numbers, if that's what you're asking. All I know is she bought her house and lives in a suite in the basement in Brentwood. She has this strict routine she lives by, and does jobs for people who need their money traced. She always has meetings with clients at the public library near her house. To keep the library happy, she makes a sizable donation every year."

Why are you telling me all of this? Lane looked at the river poking a mini-mountain range of ice up along the edge of the Bow.

"I'm telling you this because she traced proposed murder blogs back to Dr. Pierce's personal computer. We can't use the evidence, but now I'm sure we're after the right pair." Nigel glanced to his right to gauge Lane's reaction.

Before you tell him it was wrong, remember how you never revealed what you know about Uncle Tran, and how it has benefitted victims, you, and your family for years. "Is Anna in danger? If she's taking money away from ruthless people, they aren't going to be happy about it."

"I don't think so. Anna is very good. She explained that Milton has over twenty million — well, now it's down by five. She's also going after the money the Pierces have stashed away."

"What!?"

"Haven't you been reading the paper? Donations have been made to the Children's Hospital, the Red Cross..."

"Shit! It was you!"

"It was Anna. I told you, it's an ethical thing with her. She researched Milton, who publicly claimed all of the money raised in Paradise goes to support his community. She traced several private accounts in his name where the money is stashed. Anna says he's lying, she knows where the money is, he exploits the women and children in his community, and she's going after what he values most. She's getting ready to do the same with the killers. Keep watching the papers. In the next week or so you may see reports of more donations to various local charities." Nigel eased into the left lane, putting his foot down on the accelerator as they climbed out of the river valley.

"It's dangerous work." Lane watched the LRT scoot up the hill alongside them.

"She says she's very careful about being a ghost."

"I'm talking about both of you."

Nigel glanced at Lane as they crested the hill. "How so?"

"You're walking a tightrope. Be careful which side you come down on."

They travelled in silence along Bow Trail, past the golf course and condos, then up the hill into Cougar Ridge. They parked across the street from Donna's two-storey home. The chinook had eaten away at the snowdrifts on either side of the driveway. Water dripped from the tips of snowdrifts hanging from the roof. It ran down the gutters and cascaded into storm sewers. Lane pulled the phone out of his pocket and saw it was five after eleven. A white SUV pulled up and parked in Donna's driveway. She got out of the driver's side and her son, still wearing a neck brace, climbed down out of the rear seat. Lane saw him turn his back on his mother and walk to the front door.

Donna shook her head. Her shoulders sagged. She stood in her black leather coat and black high-heeled boots watching him go.

Lane climbed out of the Chev, stepping through the slick crust of a snowdrift. He leaned on the side of the car as he walked around and onto the treacherous surface of melting ice and snow. Donna turned, saw the approaching detectives, and waited with her purse hung over her shoulder. The wind plucked the edges of her red skirt. She waved at them to follow as she walked around the side of the house and back to her shop. They waited as she reached inside of her purse, took out her keys, opened the door, and turned on the lights.

Lane closed the door behind them, standing next to Nigel on the carpet.

Donna dropped her purse onto one of the chairs, took off her coat, and hung it on the door leading to the rest of the house.

Lane noted the room was nearly completed. "How's Hansen?"

"The doctor says he's doing well and the brace can come off in a week." She crossed her arms, shaking her head.

Lane waited.

Nigel asked, "What's up?"

"Cori sold their Alpha Romeo. A guy came around to Platinum, gave her a wad of cash, and drove away. About an hour later, one of the teachers from the school down the road—the school where some of the work experience kids come from—came looking for Robert. I told her to go down the hall into the back. She went. We all watched the teacher stand at the washroom door. She got really red in the face when she heard what was going on. Then she started pounding on the door. Finally, Cori and Robert came out of the washroom. There was a big screaming match. The teacher took Robert away. And Cori, she came back into the salon and gave me this look. It's hard to describe. The bitch gave me that high school look you get when one girl thinks you're fucking her boyfriend." Donna looked over her shoulder as a reflex, checking to see if her son was listening at the door. Instead they heard him clumping around upstairs. "I'm not going back to the shop. I told the contractor if he finishes this weekend I'll pay extra."

"What do you want us to do?" Lane asked.

Donna's phone rang. She moved to her right, reaching into her purse. Lane caught a glimpse of an envelope, and the brown polymer sheen of hundred-dollar bills.

Donna pulled out her phone, closing the purse. She watched the detectives as she said, "Yes, we just got back from the doctor. He says Hansen is doing well. He's still pissed because I won't let him play hockey." She listened then said, "They're here right now." She hung up. "My husband. He told me to call you. He thinks Cori and her husband are selling the cars so they can leave town. He thinks you need to know before someone else gets hurt."

"What do you think?" Lane asked.

"I think Cori is one of those people who knows exactly how to get what she wants." Donna looked past Lane at the primer on the walls. "I've got a customer coming in a few minutes."

Lane took out his phone. "I want you to put my number on speed dial."

×

Lori sat across from Lane and Nigel in their office. "McTavish phoned. He's ready. He'll have three of his crew down in the furnace room of the house tomorrow morning. They're equipped to camp out for at least twenty-four hours. Phelps will work with the caterers. Harper is handling communications and logistics. He wants you and Nigel to freelance just in case something unexpected happens. Harper's a little worried about the weather." She wore a pair of tan slacks, her leather boots, and a pink blouse.

"What's up with the weather?" Nigel asked.

Lane pointed his mouse at the weather icon. "Cold front moving in. A risk of freezing rain on Saturday."

"Harper assigned you a Jeep so you can get around if the weather doesn't cooperate." Lori checked the item off her list.

"Anything else on that list, boss?" Nigel asked.

"Yes, it says here, 'If Nigel is a pain in the ass then you have the authority to...'" Lori smiled.

Nigel exploded. "It doesn't really say that!"

Lori handed him the list.

Nigel took a look, blushed, and handed the list back.

"He also told me to tell the pair of you he needs you to be sharp tomorrow. All of the angles are covered, and now you are to go home and get some rest." Lori made an oversized check mark in the air above her list, stood up, and left the office.

×

"Sarah phoned me today." Christine manoeuvred the oversized stroller over clear sidewalks, concrete covered in ice, residential streets covered in soup. Indiana was dressed in a sleeper, stuck in a poncho, and wrapped in a blanket. His eyes were just visible where the blue toque and scarf didn't touch. They walked in winter coats and boots in the silvery half-light filtering through the thick layer of a chinook arch. Clear blue sky peeked out from under its western edge, revealing the tips of the Rocky Mountains.

Lane held Sam's leash in his left hand. A grey squirrel bounded across the top of the snow's hard crust in a neighbour's front yard. It scampered up the trunk of a poplar tree. Sam hit the end of the leash. Lane's left arm was nearly yanked out of its socket. Christine used her free hand to grab the leash. Sam danced on his rear legs.

Matt followed along behind with Dan, who said, "He likes cats and rabbits, too."

After Sam settled down except for some heavy breathing, Christine said, "It was a really weird conversation. She asked if she could see Indy, then asked if we could take him to see my mom."

Lane kept one eye out for squirrels and rabbits. The other eye watched for pickup trucks with men who looked like they were from Paradise. He leaned into the wind gusting at over thirty kilometres an hour. "You're joking."

Christine shook her head. "No, and Sarah sounded afraid."

"How old is she?" Lane asked.

"Fourteen, I think." Christine looked at her uncle. "What are you thinking?"

"I'm thinking about twenty different things right now." He looked over his shoulder to see if there was anyone behind Matt and Dan.

"Something big happening with the case?" Dan asked.

Lane nodded.

"You'll be careful?" Christine asked.

Lane spotted a bearded neighbour being pulled along by a white-breasted boxer with a blue blanket over its back. There was tension in the leash as Sam began to pull.

"Is it the serial killer?" Matt asked.

The boxer planted its front feet, staring at Sam and beginning to growl.

Lane grabbed the leash with both hands the instant before Sam hit the end of the nylon webbing. The boxer began to bark. Sam howled and barked in reply. It was a sound Lane had never heard Sam make before, a sound of wild anger. Sam became seventy-five pounds of muscle and bone fighting to get at the boxer. Lane leaned back into the leash, then reached for Sam's collar.

"What's wrong with him?" Christine asked as Matt and Dan helped Lane pull the normally playful Sam back the way they'd come.

Matt said, "There's something about that boxer that drives Sam crazy."

chapter 20

Accused Child Abductor Offers Information on Trafficking of Underage Girls

Alison Milton, accused of attempted child abduction in January, has offered to testify about the way young women are traded back and forth across the Canada–US border.

Joseph Lane, Alison Milton's legal representative, says she has "damning" evidence that Efram Milton transported girls as young as thirteen to the United States with the intent of marrying them to men who were often in their fifties and sixties. Milton recently escaped custody and is being sought by police.

Lane says, "Alison also worked as a mid-wife. She delivered a baby for a girl who had just turned fifteen. Alison Milton is willing to testify the girl was coerced into marriage with Efram Milton."

When asked if Alison Milton plans to plead guilty to the abduction charge, Mr. Lane said, "Alison's defence may reveal more about the coercive nature of her marriage."

"I wish we could take the espresso machine with us." Andrew Pierce poured fresh beans into the stainless-steel coffee grinder. "I'm taking this grinder." He turned on the machine. It growled, grinding the coffee beans into grains for the espresso machine.

"They said they wanted it furnished, so they get it furnished. We'll buy new when we get there. I was getting tired of this stuff anyway." Cori waved at the oak table and chairs. "I had my eye on a cocobolo table when we were last there." She tucked her passports into the side pocket of the tan Prada bag she had bought in New York after one of their earlier trips.

"We're ready to go?"

Cori snapped her purse shut. "All we need to do now is decide on where to go for lunch. Then I have a few things to pick up on the way."

The professor left the coffee machine for a moment, picking up a green duffle bag with black straps. He zipped it open, lifted out items, and arranged them in a line across the kitchen table. The nine-millimetre handgun was on the far left followed by blue coveralls, surgical gloves, white booties, and hairnets. The FlexiCuffs were next, then a package of wipes and a spray bottle of bleach. "It's all here. I'll put it by the garage door so we don't forget it."

"Remember, I've got my eye on those shoes," Cori said.

×

Lane and Nigel were dressed causally in clothing designed for warmth and freedom of movement. They listened while Lori checked off points on the fingers of her left hand. "McTavish's team is in place. She let them in this morning. Phelps is already down at the caterer's getting to know everyone, becoming part of the crew. The surveillance teams are in place."

"She?" Lane asked.

Lori nodded. "The lady of the house."

"What about the husband?" Lane asked.

"Out of town apparently." Lori saw the frown on Lane's face. "What?"

"They said five." Lane looked at the screen on his desk.

"What?" Nigel asked.

"When I overheard the pair of them talking at the theatre, they said five."

×

"You sure you don't have these in a nine?" Cori handed back the red shoes with red musical notes inlaid in white soles.

The sales person, who might have been eighteen, shook her head, tucking back a wayward strand of black curly hair.

"I want you to go downstairs and check again." Cori stuffed the too-small shoe into the box, thrusting the box at the clerk.

Andrew stood behind her, holding both of their winter coats and her purse.

×

"It looks like you may not have air cover tonight." Harper stood inside Lane's office. The detectives and Lori were going over the final details of surveillance and hostage scenarios.

Lane leaned back in his chair. He rubbed the muscles at the front of his rib cage. *He looks worried.*

Harper said, "The weather forecast is calling for rain, a wind shift to the north, freezing rain, then snow."

Lane nodded. "We need to make sure we have the right ground vehicles."

"I'll make it happen." Harper left.

Lane looked out the window. The normally sharp edge of the chinook arch was looking ragged. He checked a Canadian flag tugging at the pole. "The wind's shifting."

×

"Uncle Lane?" Christine's voice was tense.

Is Indy okay? "What's happened?" He drove south on Crowchild Trail, easing onto the right lane, taking the ramp to Marda Loop.

"I got another weird call from my half-sister Sarah. She said goodbye."

Lane could hear Dan in the background. *Milton's making his run.* "Call Lori and ask her to put you in touch with the RCMP. Tell them you have information that Milton is going to head south into the United States so he can disappear into one of the polygamist compounds. Also tell her it's human trafficking."

"What?"

Lane said, "Call Lori and explain she needs to talk with Harper. He'll get in touch with the RCMP. It's a suspected case of human trafficking. Then tell Lori about Sarah and Milton. Okay?"

Christine's voice shook. "Okay."

×

Lane sipped coffee at Phil and Sebastian's at Marda Loop between Crowchild Trail and Mount Royal. He watched the cars going past. Their wipers shuddered back and forth, pushing the mist away. White and purple globes hanging on a nearby tree bobbed in the wind.

"Climate change." Nigel looked at the coffee shop's cubbyhole wall stocked with clear glass jars of coffee beans.

"Fucking weather," a man said as he paid for his coffee. "Can always count on Calgary. The weather is shit."

"What do you think?" Nigel sipped from a paper cup. He wore dark clothing so he would be less conspicuous if they needed nighttime camouflage.

Lane wore a black shirt and pants. A black parka hung off the back of his chair. "If the temperature drops all of a sudden, the soupy stuff on the roads will freeze, and the rain will make the driving more like skating."

"Icy roads are always fun." Nigel looked at his phone. "It's almost nine."

"The party will probably break up soon because people will be worried about the roads. This place is closing. We'd better get refills." Lane's phone rang. He pulled it out of his shirt pocket. "Hello?"

McTavish said, "The suspects have left the party, headed north."

"Got it." Lane pressed *End*, stuffed the phone in his shirt pocket, put on his coat, and grabbed his coffee. He stepped outside into a north wind turning his breath into smoke, carrying it south as he walked across the street to the Jeep. His ears began to freeze. When he reached the other side of the street, he threw the coffee in a trashcan, zipped up his jacket, lifted the collar around his ears, and tucked in his chin.

Nigel got in the driver's seat, started the engine, and turned the wipers on. They swiped at the ice on the windshield, doing nothing to clear the opaque surface. Lane climbed in the passenger side, turned the heat to defrost, grabbed the scraper out of the back seat, got out, and began to chip away at the ice on the windshield. His phone rang. He opened his jacket and pulled the phone out of his shirt pocket, turning his back on the wind. Nigel tried to clear the front glass with windshield-washer antifreeze. The smell of alcohol hung in the air.

McTavish said, "They've stopped at their home. I'll keep you informed." He hung up.

Lane tucked his phone away and opened the door, stuffing the scraper behind the seat. He looked at the expanding half moons of clear windshield. His phone rang again.

McTavish said, "They're on the move again, heading your way along 33rd. They are wearing dark clothing and driving a grey BMW X5 with licence plate DR DETH. Got that?"

"Confirmed. The tail?" Lane asked.

"Black Ford pickup. Licence RUF-4387."

"Got it." Lane hung up, turning to Nigel. "They're headed our way in the grey SUV. The tail is a black Ford pickup."

Nigel nodded, alternating between the side mirror and the rear-view. "Here they come."

Lane caught a glimpse of the X5 and Cori's platinum-blonde hair. She held a phone against her right ear. Seconds later, a black Ford pickup passed them.

Lane checked the Ford's plate. Nigel pulled out, following. "Glad they gave us the Jeep with the studded winter tires."

They drove west on 33rd, crossing over Crowchild Trail as the rain fell, freezing against the top half of the Jeep's windshield. Nigel leaned right to see through the bottom half of the windshield. Lane crouched to watch out of a spot the size of a dessert plate, slowly expanding as the engine warmed and the heater caught up. By the time they approached a Co-Op grocery store on their right, the heater was winning the battle against the freezing rain.

Lane's phone rang. He pulled it out of his shirt pocket. "Lane."

Lori said, "A 911 call just came in. A report of shots fired at Cori and Andrew Pierce's address."

Lane looked ahead, seeing the taillights of the pickup light up. He turned right. Nigel took over the lead tail on the Pierce BMW. It turned north on Sarcee Trail and into the teeth of the wind.

Lane asked, "Was the caller female? Did she identify herself?"

Lori said, "Yes and no."

Lane turned to Nigel. "Remember those Pierce blog titles?"

Nigel nodded.

"Was one of them about creating a diversion?"

Nigel said, "Yep."

Lane felt a gust of wind push against the Jeep. "Send two units to the house and get back to me as soon as possible with what they find."

Lori said, "Will do." She hung up.

Lane's phone rang again. He looked at the face, recognized McTavish's number, and put the phone to his ear. "Yes."

McTavish said, "Tell us where we can back you up. We're headed parallel along 45th Street. The suspect took a long look at us in his rear-view. Keep this line open and update me."

"Okay." Lane watched the BMW surge ahead. Nigel put his foot to the floor, still losing ground.

Lane blinked, shaking his head, tapping Nigel's right arm. *I hope I've got this right.* "Hang back. I know where they're going. Andrew said it's a two-fer. Cori said the total would be five. The woman in Mount Royal is one." *And Donna has an envelope full of hundred-dollar bills to pay the contractor tomorrow. Cori must know about it.* Lane spoke into the phone. "They're headed for Cougar Ridge." He gave McTavish the address.

Lane squinted to keep the taillights of the grey BMW in view. The rain turned to snow; visibility dropped to less than one hundred metres. The wipers worked at full speed, the detectives staring into the white headlight glare, searching for the BMW. Above them they saw faces in windows as the LRT flashed overhead. They passed under the 17th Avenue Bridge. Momentary calm. They came out from under the bridge and back into the blizzard's breath.

"I can't see them." Nigel shifted into a lower gear. The engine roared.

Lane hung on. They reached the lights at Bow Trail. The light was red. The Pierce BMW wasn't in sight. Nigel waited for a break in traffic, turning left against the red and up the curve of the hill. The Jeep's traction control kicked in and out.

Less than five minutes later they pulled up in front of Donna's house. Across the street a thin layer of snow coated the roof and rear window of the BMW with the DR DETH licence plate. Nigel parked in front of it.

Lane saw fresh footprints in the snow. He got out and followed the trail to the back of the house. There was a hole smashed in the glass of the door to Donna's shop. Lane tried the handle. It opened. He turned to Nigel, bringing the thumb and pinky finger of his right hand to his ear, handing him the phone. Nigel nodded, taking Lane's phone. He stepped inside, seeing the open door at the back of Donna's salon. He slipped on the floor. He looked down at his snow-covered shoes and patches of wet on the linoleum. *I need quiet, and I can't slip.* He placed the right toe on the heel of the left foot, pulling his left foot out, then freeing his right. He padded to the bottom of the stairs, noting the carpet, pulled out his Glock, eased the slide back, and put a round into the chamber. He felt his way upstairs.

He heard the professor's voice. "Let's make this easy. We're here for the money."

Lane reached the top of the stairs, turning right along a hallway leading to the kitchen. It was on his left with the family room on the right. Beyond that, a door led to the deck. Andrew and Cori wore matching blue overalls, standing side by side with their backs to Lane. Both wore white hairnets and booties. Beyond them Lane could see Donna and her husband in kitchen chairs. Both had their waists, wrists, and ankles wrapped with silver duct tape. Cori moved away from them with the roll of tape in her right hand. Donna spotted Lane, then looked to her left. *She's telling me her boys are to my right.*

Lane tapped his index finger on the trigger guard of his Glock.

Cori said, "I'll ask once more. Then someone will die if you don't answer. Where did you stash the cash?"

Lane moved forward, seeing the handgun in Andrew Pierce's right hand. He stood to the right and about two metres from Donna and her husband. Pierce raised his weapon, holding it in both hands, aiming at Donna.

Lane felt his arm bringing the Glock to bear on the professor. *Remember to breathe.*

"Kill the oldest boy," Cori said.

Lane took in the scene, his training making the moves automatic. He cupped his left hand under his right. *I have a clear line of fire.*

The professor began to swing the handgun to his right.

"No!" Donna said. "It's in the upstairs laundry closet!" Pierce hesitated.

"Kill him anyway." Cori smiled.

"Police!" Lane forced himself to take a long, slow breath while aiming for the professor's torso.

Andrew Pierce turned toward the detective. Lane noticed the man's eyes were wide with wild excitement. The detective moved his finger onto the trigger, centring the sight on the man's sternum.

BOOM! Pierce fired. One hundred sixty decibels were confined to the kitchen and family room. Lane didn't hear the bullet hit the wall twenty centimetres from his head. He squeezed the trigger of his Glock, feeling the shock of recoil. BOOM! One of the boys screamed. Pierce looked surprised, touching his chest with his left fingertips. His right still held the gun, pointing to the ceiling, then lowering. *Is he wearing Kevlar?* Lane aimed at the hole in the professor's chest, squeezing. BOOM! The spent shell casing bounced off the wall, hitting the back of Lane's right hand. His nose filled with the musky stink of burnt oil and powder. He saw two holes in the centre of the man's coveralls, yet the professor was still standing. Pierce aimed at the detective. Lane squeezed the trigger.

BOOM! A hole appeared where the professor's right eye had been. His body folded, flopping onto the floor.

Cori moved to her left. Lane saw the box cutter in her right hand. "Drop the knife." He levelled his gun at her chest.

She dropped the yellow knife, pointing at the professor. "He forced me into this."

"Bullshit!" Donna leaned forward to stand, falling back into the chair. "Cut me loose! I'll kill you, you fucking cow!"

Lane heard a child crying.

He stepped further into the room, looking to his right. Hansen sat on a black leather couch. His eyes were open wide as were his younger brother's. Both boys had their hands tied together with white plastic cuffs. The younger boy wailed, staring at Dr. Pierce's twitching right foot. Blood stained the carpet. The boys lifted their feet up onto the couch. One had a dark wet stain in his crotch. Lane walked into the room, picking up Andrew's weapon.

"Cut me the fuck loose! She's getting away!" Donna said.

Lane looked left, seeing Cori stepping out the door to the deck. Then he heard her feet pounding as she ran. He felt a hand on his shoulder. "You okay?" Nigel stepped up beside him. Lane looked left at his partner.

Donna said, "We're okay! Get Cori!"

Lane holstered his Glock, ejected the clip from Pierce's handgun, then the round from the chamber, setting the gun on the counter. He experienced an instant of absolute clarity as he made eye contact with his partner. "You got this?"

Nigel nodded, holding his phone up in his left hand. "Backup is almost here. I'll phone for an ambulance."

"Give me the keys." Lane felt them being placed in his palm, detached from the touch of metal and plastic against flesh. He turned and went out the front door, then walked down the front steps and to the front edge of the garage. The BMW's starter whined. The engine caught. He saw Cori behind the windshield, the wipers swiping snow away from the glass. The V–8 engine roared. Cori pulled away.

Lane ran for the Jeep. It wasn't until his right foot wrapped its toes onto the accelerator that he remembered where he'd left his shoes.

He followed Cori south, then west. *She has the advantage on performance. The snow and ice will even things out.*

Cori slid around a corner, driving over a stop sign, heading west along a straight stretch of road. Lane rounded the corner, pressing the accelerator. The BMW pulled away.

Blue, red, and white lights flashed ahead. Cori's brake lights came on. Lane heard a siren. A black-and-white police SUV passed them going in the opposite direction. Cori turned left. He caught a glimpse of a road sign: Old Banff Coach Road. He remembered being eight or nine in the back seat of his father's black Cadillac, feeling sick after a series of sharp turns. He pressed down on the accelerator. The Jeep skidded, swaying, skipping, and gripping over patches of snow and ice. *The plows and sanders won't hit this stretch of road for hours.* He backed off the pedal while Cori accelerated.

A radio or television tower rose on his right, its guy wires stretching up into the storm. Then it was gone. Cori's taillights disappeared. A sign appeared in a world turned white: Artist Viewpoint. Then he saw a yellow sign warning of an upcoming turn and eased off the accelerator. The Jeep's headlights focused into a cone where white snowflakes were illuminated, sweeping out of the dark on one side, into the night on the other.

Another yellow warning sign. Another turn. The Jeep skidded. One tire found a patch of gravel. Lane steered out of the turn. Up ahead, another ninety–degree turn and a pair of red eyes staring back out of the white and the night. He eased his foot off the accelerator. The Jeep skidded, then recovered.

The BMW brake lights came closer. Lane put his right foot on the brake pedal. He pulled off onto the edge of the road, turning on his four-way flashers, shifted into neutral, pulled the emergency brake, and reached to pick his phone out of his pocket. *Nigel has it!*

Lane opened the door, pulling the Glock out of its holster. He looked left and right, then into the white. Seeing no halo of approaching headlights, he crossed the road. He slid down into the ditch, balancing with his left hand, holding the Glock high. His right foot stepped on a walnut-sized piece of gravel and he winced. *Shit!*

The BMW was on its roof, hung up in a barbed-wire fence, its passenger side against a trce. He pulled a flashlight out of his pocket, shining it on the driver's door. His Glock followed the light. Airbags hung down from the steering wheel, obscuring half the shattered driver's window. The driver's door began to open. Cori tumbled out on her hands and knees. "Who are you?"

"Lie face down. Put your hands on the back of your head." Lane aimed the light in her eyes.

"I'm the victim here. Andrew told me he would kill me if I didn't do what he said."

"Lie face down!" He held the Glock out front of the light so she could see its lethal black silhouette.

Cori did as shc was told.

"I am a police officer. You are being placed under arrest."

Lane came closer, crouching, putting a knee in the small of her back, holstering the Glock, grabbing her left wrist with his right hand, reaching for his handcuffs. He locked her right hand first, then her left, lifting her to her feet.

"I'm cut." She wiped her chin on her shoulder.

I don't give a fuck! "Walk to the road."

"I think the airbag broke one of my ribs." She walked ahead. Lane saw she still wore her white booties over a pair of lace-up boots.

He put his right hand in the small of her back, pushing her up out of the ditch and onto the road. She slipped on the black ice, falling to her knees. "You made me fall."

Socks are better on this. "Get up."

He pulled her up by her right elbow. They walked across the road to the Jeep. "Stop." He held the cuffs with his right hand, pushing her up against the side of the Jeep, and opened the door with his left. "Back up." He grabbed the chain joining the cuffs, pulling her backwards so he could sit in the driver's seat. He pulled his feet in, then felt for the heater control. He turned the hot air onto his feet. He switched hands with the cuffs, pulling out his Glock with his right hand.

"I'm cold. Let me sit inside," Cori said.

Lane heard the pleading in her tone, but he also heard the calculation. *You remind me of my siblings.* "You'll be inside soon enough." He watched the snow gathering on her shoulders and hair. Then he remembered her face — that smile of anticipation, that tone of command — when she told her husband to kill one of Donna's boys. He looked at the Glock. He looked at her, remembering the bodies in the Randall home. *She might be able to get away with this. I could put this gun to the back of her neck, and she will never hurt another person.*

"I want a lawyer."

Lane flashed back to the startled look on Andrew Pierce's face when the bullets hit his chest. He felt the weight of the weapon in his hand, the power of it. "You have that right, and you will have the others read to you momentarily." *I could put the gun to the base of her skull, angle the barrel up into the brain, and squeeze the trigger. I already killed the husband. It was easier than I thought it would be. I'm a killer because of this one.* Lane stared at the gun in his hand, seeing his forefinger across the trigger guard. Blue-and-white lights flashed, illuminating the inside of the Jeep's cab in an eerie alternating dance. Lane looked left over his shoulder. The headlights of the approaching vehicle flashed on and off. Then another vehicle's flashing lights approached. The first vehicle stopped. The headlights were almost a metre off of the ground. *McTavish is here.*

The driver's door opened. "Everything under control?" McTavish asked before he stepped out in front of his head-lights.

"She's cuffed. She needs her rights read to her. Take her, please." Lane watched as McTavish took hold of Cori's elbow. Another officer stepped into the glare of the headlights.

Cori said, "This man shot my husband."

McTavish turned to the officer beside him. "Wait for a moment. I want to be a witness as you read her rights."

Lane saw the officer was wearing his blues underneath a nylon jacket. The officer looked at Lane, then took Cori by the elbow, reading her rights. McTavish nodded when the officer was finished, and took Cori back to the pickup.

McTavish held out his hand. "ASIRT is on its way. So is Harper. I need your weapon."

Lane pointed his Glock at the dash and ejected the clip, then the round in the chamber. The slide was open. McTavish pulled a bag out of his pocket. He took the bits of the Glock one by one, placing them in the bag. "What can I get you?"

Lane tried to smile. He shrugged instead. He heard a voice. "A cup of coffee and my shoes." His voice sounded vague, unfamiliar. "Someone needs to give the Randall family a call."

chapter 21

Fugitive Polygamist Arrested at the Border

Canadian border authorities arrested Efram Milton, the self-proclaimed prophet of Paradise, at the Chief Mountain Border Crossing in southern Alberta. Milton was attempting to cross into Montana.

Two females, aged thirteen and fourteen, with Milton at the time of his arrest, were taken into protective custody. Initial reports suggest the girls were being transported to a polygamist community in Utah.

The RCMP confiscated four firearms, including a Heckler and Kock 9-mm handgun, a shotgun, and two Winchesters. They also found a large duffle bag filled with an unspecified amount of cash. A second male was arrested at the scene. His name has not been released.

Milton escaped custody in Calgary and was the subject of a province-wide manhunt. He was remanded in custody and will face a series of new charges in a Calgary court on Monday.

Arthur waited at the door as Lane was dropped off mid-morning. He hugged his partner in the doorway. Lane kicked off his shoes. After Arthur released him, Lane sat down and peeled off his still-damp socks.

"What do you need?" Arthur asked.

"A bath." Lane took off his winter jacket and hung it up. *It's amazing. Here I am doing the usual things as if nothing has changed.*

"No questions?" Arthur put his hand on Lane's shoulder.

Lane tried to smile. "That would be nice." He went upstairs, got a change of clothes from the bedroom, walked into the main bathroom, and locked the door. He ran the tub, got undressed, and got in. Every time the phone rang, he let his head fall back under the water, covering his ears. He got out when his feet and hands had started to wrinkle.

He dried himself off, put on a T-shirt and sweatpants, and went to bed.

chapter 22

This is Shazia Wajdan outside the home of University of Calgary professor Andrew Pierce.

Dr. Andrew Stephen Pierce, age thirty-five, was shot and killed by a member of the Calgary Police Service in the neighbourhood of Cougar Ridge late Saturday night.

At a news conference Sunday afternoon, CPS announced that the Alberta Serious Incident Response Team will investigate the officer-involved shooting.

CUT TO CHIEF JIM SIMPSON, CALGARY POLICE SERVICE
"The ASIRT team has interviewed the officers involved as well as witnesses at the scene. ASIRT is in the process of investigating the sequence of events leading up to this fatality."

Chief Simpson confirms that Cori Mallory Pierce, wife of Dr. Pierce, has been arrested and is in custody.

When asked to confirm reports of hostages being involved, Chief Simpson would not comment, noting that the investigation is in its early stages.

Colleagues of Dr. Pierce expressed shock at his death.

CUT TO DR. EDGAR WHILES, DEAN OF EDUCATION
"He was such a vibrant man and active in the social life of the university. It's shocking that he should die in such a violent manner."

A check of Dr. Pierce's Facebook account reveals several entries in which he expresses concern over his safety.

When asked about the possibility of overturning the conviction of Byron Thomas, who was found guilty of an earlier murder, Chief Simpson said that the process is already underway.

Shazia Wajdan, CBC News, Calgary.

Lane woke to the sound of Indiana crying. He turned over in the dark, looking at the clock. *Eleven o'clock. I've slept more than twelve hours!* He rolled out of bed, stuffed his feet into sandals, and moved downstairs. At the bottom of the stairs he looked to the right, where Arthur snored as he slept on the couch under a white comforter. Dan was in the kitchen holding the baby, trying to warm a bottle under the tap.

"Let me take him," Lane said. Dan handed over Indy, who stopped crying for a moment, opened his eyes, then began to cry again. Dan tried the formula on his wrist and handed the bottle to Lane. The crying stopped when the bottle touched Indy's mouth.

"You slept for a long time," Dan said.

Lane nodded, feeling Indy's warmth, seeing a tiny hand touch the glass of the bottle. "Go back to sleep. I've got this."

"You sure?" Dan put his hand on Lane's shoulder.

Lane smiled. "Yes." He sat down on a kitchen chair while Dan went downstairs. Lane held the bottle for the baby while studying Indy's open eyes, thick black hair, and round face. Lane stood up, looked out the window, saw snow falling. The flakes were loonie-sized. He leaned up over the sink and close to the window. Snowflakes created a halo around the streetlamp. The roof of their car appeared to have ten centimetres of snow on top. "What do you think of all this snow?"

Indy released his bottle. There was a hissing of air. Lane set the bottle on the counter and moved Indy up onto his shoulder. The detective began to pat the baby's back. He could smell formula, baby shampoo, urine, and the faint scent of gun oil on his hands.

Lane started to move around the kitchen and dining room as he patted Indy's back, not quite able to escape the scent of gun oil and flashbacks of Dr. Pierce's open-eyed stare as he lay at the feet of Donna's sons. *I wonder how they're doing?*

Indy burped. Lane looked sideways at the baby, and he burped again. "Glad you enjoyed that." Lane sat down and continued to feed Indy until the baby fell asleep.

chapter 23

Lane and Sam walked along the snow-covered sidewalk. The snow muffled noises except for the crunch of Lane's boots as they compressed the white. His phone rang. Sam watched the detective fumble for it. *I should throw it away.* Instead, Lane looked at the face of the phone, recognized the number, and pressed the green with his thumb.

"I have some news for you," Nigel said.

"All right." Lane kept walking. Sam kept pulling the leash, and the detective kept yanking back.

"Forensics has been working overtime on the Pierce BMW. An external hard drive was sent to Nebal, who took about fifteen minutes to find her way into some video files. The professor and his wife kept records of six different crime scenes, a total of twelve homicides. The videos show Cori Pierce was an active participant, most often an instigator. Evidence is being prepared for the Crown Prosecutor. They also recovered the bullet Andrew Pierce fired at you. It's intact and being processed as we speak." Nigel waited. "I thought you'd want to know."

"Thank you."

"What are you doing?"

"Walking Sam the dog." Lane saw a squirrel running along the top of a fence. Sam pulled on the leash.

"You did your job. You saved the lives of the innocents."

I killed a man. I should feel something. I just feel numb. "Please call if there are more developments."

"One other thing."

The squirrel climbed a tree, looking down and chattering at Sam. "What's that?"

"We found two empty blood bags in the back of the BMW. It's been type matched to the blood spatter at the Pierce home. It's also a type match to Cori and Andrew. DNA analysis will take a little longer. It looks like the social media entries made by Andrew, the 911 call, and blood evidence were designed to divert us. We were meant to assume the Pierces were either killed or kidnapped. That way, they hoped to create confusion so they could disappear while sending us on a wild goose chase."

Lane spotted a white jackrabbit bounding down the street. He gripped the leash with his free hand the instant before the dog lunged. "What did the Randalls say?"

"They thanked me. They said they would get back to us after they had time to digest the information."

"Thanks."

"You all right?"

"Sam's after a rabbit. Gotta go." He pressed *End*, stuffing the phone in a pocket and grabbing the leash with both hands. At the end of the block, they crossed the street to the pathway running below the edge of soccer fields and a baseball diamond bordered by chain-link fence. Lane watched Sam sniff the air. The dog stopped. Lane looked left. About forty metres above them, at the edge of the fields set up on a plateau, three coyotes travelled single file. They glanced down at Lane and Sam without stopping. The hunters appeared comfortable in their thick grey winter coats. They puffed frosty breath into the air, trotting along in search of the jackrabbits, mice, voles, and squirrels living in the neighbourhood. They turned left through a gate in the chain-link fence and were gone. *Just three hunters out for a walk.* He looked at his dog. "Not much different from us, eh Sam?"

When they got home, there was a Cadillac Escalade parked out front. The licence plate read LLAGETS. "Fuck."

Maybe I should just keep walking. Sam began to limp. *Got ice stuck in your paws?*

He took Sam around to the back door, removed the leash, and shut the gate behind him. His right elbow ached from being turned inside out by Sam. Lane went around to the front door, climbed the steps, opened the door, and stepped inside. He heard conversation coming up from downstairs as he leaned down to untie his boots.

"He's absolutely gorgeous!" Lola's voice was in full fog-horn mode.

Lane hung up his coat. *This is the last thing I need right now.*

"He's three weeks old now." John's voice carried up the stairs.

Lane went to the top of the stairs. *I may need a drink or four before this night is over.*

"Since we haven't had an invitation, we decided to drop over," Lola said.

"Are you the one who wanted to change the colour of my sister's skin?" Alex, who sat next to her sister on the couch, stood up, taking Indy from Lola.

Maybe this won't be so bad. Thank you, Alex. Lane stepped down the stairs and onto the family room floor. *Saturday night I wore socks when I killed a man.*

John was across the room in an armchair. He stood up, glaring at Alex.

Lola waved at him. "Oh, sit down. I had that coming." She looked at Dan, then at Lane. "I am asking to see Indy."

Arthur gave Lane a worried frown.

There is no self-help guru who tells people exactly what to say to a man who just shot and killed someone.

Christine touched her son's cheek, looking at Lane. "What do you say, Uncle?"

Lane sat on the arm of Arthur's chair. "Not my call."

"She respects your opinion," Dan said.

Lane felt a hand on his back. *You've always got my back, Arthur.* "A child needs family." He looked at a smiling Lola. "Christine and Dan always have the final say. They must be respected as the parents of the child."

Lola frowned.

The room held its breath.

Alex leaned forward to say something. Christine put her hand on her sister's arm. Alex clamped her mouth closed.

Lane watched the worried look on John's face.

Lola turned to Lane, who met her gaze.

Indiana farted, making a *putt-putt* sound. The volume wasn't remarkable. The start-to-finish time was. Matt was the first to laugh. "You're my hero, Indy!"

Lola stood, waiting for the laughter to subside. "We came here because I have an apology to make and this." She reached into her purse, pulling out an envelope. "The two of you deserve a nice wedding if it's what you choose." She held up the envelope. "This is yours. No strings attached. It's airfare, accommodation for ten, and a wedding ceremony in Cuba."

Lane watched Lola. *She's not crying, not even close to it.* He wiped at his eyes even as he felt rage boiling.

Dan said, "We're not for sale."

Lola turned to him. "I said no strings attached." She handed the envelope to Christine, then looked at John. "We'd better go."

John stood.

Arthur said, "You're staying for supper."

Lane glared at him. Arthur glared right back. Lane sensed the room turning to look at him. He felt tears rolling down his cheeks. He wiped at them with the back of his hand. Someone stood to put an arm around his shoulder. It was Matt.

"What's the matter with him?" Lola asked.

Matt said, "It's a delayed reaction. He shot a man on Saturday night. We were warned this might happen."

Lane tried to speak, but his voice was choked off by emotion.

Arthur said, "Chief Simpson called and told us there will be help available, because it's hard to predict how an officer will react under these circumstances."

Christine continued. "So we contacted Dr. Alexandre, who predicted Uncle Lane would probably internalize the experience, but the shock would wear off and then this might happen."

Dan said, "We were told to be ready just in case."

"To be there for him," Arthur said.

Lola said, "You were the one who killed Pierce? We knew someone was killing off the Nine Bottles. It was you who saved that family?"

"And now he's paying the price for it," Arthur said.

Matt got close to Lane's ear. "Nigel phoned. He feels guilty, because he thinks he froze when he should have fired."

In his mind's eye, Lane replayed the scene. The angles of fire. The locations of Donna and her family. Through tears he caught Lola's brief smile of triumph. The words on the note stuck to Nigel's computer screen came back to him: VENEER & PLASTIC, PLASTIC & VENEER. He said, "I need to make a call." Lane got up, climbing the stairs to the master bedroom.

✕

Nigel and Anna sat across from each other at her usual spot in the library. It was five o'clock.

"So you were there?" Anna looked out into the library proper.

Nigel nodded. "I came through the door connecting the kitchen to the pantry and laundry room. The professor shot at my partner, who returned fire."

"What did you do?"

"Nothing. I froze."

Anna looked at her laptop. "I want to show you something." She lifted the screen, tapping a key.

Nigel leaned over. He could smell the gentle scent of strawberry soap and shampoo. Anna turned the screen so he could read the numbers. Nigel asked, "That's how much the professor and his wife had stashed away?"

Anna nodded. "And this is real estate in Mexico."

"So they made murder profitable."

"For a while."

Nigel sat back. "What are you going to do with it?"

"I like the Children's Hospital. What do you think?"

Nigel nodded. His phone rang. He picked it out of his pocket, reading the number. "I have to take this." He pressed a button.

"Nigel? We need to talk. Can you come over?" Lane asked.

"When?"

"Now."

×

Nigel walked in the front door, saw the assortment of shoes and boots just inside, and was greeted by a smiling, round-faced, balding man with Mediterranean features saying, "Glad you could make it. Hope you like pizza."

Lane appeared. He was wearing a black T-shirt and dress pants, and had a baby tucked in his arm. "Arthur, this is Nigel."

Nigel hesitated for a moment, unsure if he should shake hands, and was instead engulfed in a hug from Arthur. "Good to meet you."

The house smelled of tomato sauce, pepperoni, ham, and pineapple. A large dog arrived, promptly sticking his nose in Nigel's crotch.

"Sorry." Arthur grabbed the dog's collar, pulling him back. "Sam, behave yourself."

Lane said, "Come on in. Hope you like pizza."

"I'm not really hungry." Nigel took off his coat. Arthur hung it up.

"We need to talk." Lane went to sit on the recliner in the front room. He looked down at the sleeping baby as he waited for Nigel to sit on the couch. The sound of conversation came up the stairs from the family room.

"I'm sorry. I didn't realize you have guests." Nigel moved to get up.

Lane stopped him by opening his free hand. "Please. I need to know what you saw on Saturday night. I need to know if what I saw, what I did —"

Nigel took a long, shuddering breath.

Lane waited.

"I came up the stairs after you. Then I went around to the left to flank you. There was a passageway from the laundry room through the pantry and into the kitchen. I had my gun out. I saw Cori and Andrew Pierce. Donna and her husband sat in front of them. Cori told Andrew to shoot one of the boys. I could just see the kids' feet because they sat on the couch along the wall next to you."

Nigel took a breath. "I just stood there and froze as the professor turned. Then you said, 'Police!' I saw him fire. There were three more shots. He fell down. You stepped into my field of vision, told Cori to drop the knife. Then she took off out the door."

Lane nodded. His eyes did a thousand-metre stare. Indiana kept his head nestled up against the detective's chest. "Thank you."

"For what? I didn't do anything. Couldn't do anything." Nigel's chin fell to his chest.

Lane said, "I'm sorry about the boys. That they had to see a man shot in front of them. I couldn't live with myself if anyone in Donna's family had been shot. From your position, if you had fired, it's very likely Donna, or her husband, or both would have been hit. It was your training. Remember? Use your weapon as the last option. You did what your training taught you to do. You didn't have a clear field of fire, but I did. I've been thinking about this over and over again. I think I can live with killing Andrew Pierce. I don't think I could live with myself if any of Donna's family had been killed." Lane looked down at Indy, pulling the baby away from himself and seeing the wet patch on his T-shirt. "I'm going to have to change the baby."

"I thought I'd let you down." Nigel lifted his head.

Lane stood up. "Just the opposite, in fact. Go grab a plate and some pizza. I'll get the little guy a clean diaper and a new outfit."

chapter 24

This is Shazia Wajdan with Donna Liu, eyewitness to the shooting of Dr. Andrew Pierce.

Ms. Liu, you have something you wanted to say?

CUT TO DONNA LIU "I was there. I heard what was said. I saw what happened."

Will you describe it for us?

CUT BACK TO DONNA LIU "Pierce and his wife broke into our house and taped me and my husband to chairs. They wanted some cash I had on hand to pay a contractor. Cori Pierce told her husband to shoot one of my boys. The detective must have come up the basement stairs, because he told the doctor to stop. Pierce shot at the detective. The detective shot back. He saved my boys. He saved us."

Is there anything you wanted to add?

CUT BACK TO DONNA LIU "On social media, some people are saying Pierce was a victim and a good professor. I was there. He was going to kill us."

Today, Cori Mallory Pierce, Dr. Andrew Pierce's widow, was charged with four counts of murder in the deaths of Robert and Elizabeth Randall and Megan and Douglas Newsome. She was also charged with four counts of unlawful confinement. She entered a plea of not guilty. A police spokesperson said more charges are expected to be laid against Ms. Pierce in the coming weeks.

Shazia Wajdan, CBC News, Calgary.

Nigel met Anna at Peppino's Italian Restaurant in Kensington. A red wool winter jacket hung off the back of her chair. She wore black slacks, a white blouse, and tall black-leather boots, and was sipping a coffee. He almost didn't recognize her without a hat and her multicoloured steampunk glasses. He also noticed every male in the restaurant making covert and not-so-covert glances in her direction.

She waved as he entered, pulling out the chair next to her. "I already ordered you a coffee."

Nigel took off his purple jacket, hanging it on the back of the chair before sitting down.

"You look good in purple." She watched him over the top of her cup as she sipped. Nigel caught a whiff of chocolate and her gentle citrus perfume.

He pulled at the cuffs of his new shirt. "I was surprised when I got your call. We usually meet —"

"— in the library. That's what I wanted to talk with you about." She nodded at the counter as the woman behind set a cup of coffee on the display case. "Your coffee is ready."

Nigel got up and grabbed his coffee.

Anna stared at her coffee as she spoke. "I needed to talk with you about something."

"Did the guys from Paradise trace you?" Nigel looked over his shoulder and out onto the street.

"Nothing like that." She waved her hand in front of her face.

"What's the matter?"

"Just listen."

Nigel sat back, watching Anna as she made eye contact, then looked away, and said, "When I was ten, the school got me to talk with a psychologist. Her name was Laura something. She had this nasty bullying personality. A couple of the kids saw her before I did, and they warned the rest of us. Anyway, I'd done some reading on Asperger's Syndrome.

Some of the other kids were diagnosed with it, and I was curious. I tried out some of the Asperger symptoms on her. The repetitive behaviours really got her attention. It was like this game I played with her. She'd ask a question, and I'd respond the way a kid with Asperger's would. The psychologist fell for it, and so did the psychiatrist I saw after that. Then the teachers started treating me differently. So I played along, because I found they would leave me alone. If they didn't, I'd put on a performance to make them back off. After a while, they let me do more or less whatever I wanted as long as I was quiet."

Nigel picked up his coffee, taking a sip.

"Anyway, it just got easier. I wasn't into the junior high or high school social scenes. It was like putting on a character, a role, and it became comfortable. There was always so much drama in school, so much emotion. It was a way of coping with it and keeping myself insulated from it. You've been my friend through most of that, and I wanted you to know."

Nigel watched her eyes when they dropped to study the coffee remaining in her cup. He opened his mouth, then closed it.

She lifted her eyes. "Well?"

He opened his mouth again, taking a long breath to go over the words he planned to say. "So you're an introvert, that's what you're saying?"

"And I like being an introvert, but I also like being your friend, and friends should —"

"— be able to finish each other's sentences?"

Anna smiled. "More or less."

"I guess I'm interested in what you mean by more."

Her smile got wider. "So you do understand what I'm saying."

✕

Lane wore a grey suit; Arthur, black. Christine wore black jeans and a tan blouse with a yellow scarf under a black coat. As they passed, all eyes, from the secretaries to the lawyers, turned to watch them pass.

"Which one is it?" Christine asked.

"Probably the one at the end. It's my dad's old office." *How many years has it been?* Lane read the names on the doors as they passed. *So much heavy dark wood. Feels ominous, cloistered, almost church like. I guess that's the intent.*

"This place needs a decorator," Arthur said.

They came to the end of the hall, standing outside a heavy oak door with *Joseph Lane, Q.C., A.O.E.* embossed in gold.

Arthur knocked. The door opened a few seconds later. Joseph Lane stood with his silver hair, white shirt, knotted full Windsor red tie, and blue pinstriped suit. "Hello. Right on time!" His voice was full of bonhomie as he shook their hands, gesturing for them to sit around the table across from the oak desk with elephant-sized legs. Lane noted the embossed JL on the cuffs of his brother's tailor-made shirt.

They sat down in leather wingback chairs around the polished oak table. Christine sat back in her chair and crossed one leg over the other, waiting. As if on cue, a secretary arrived carrying a tray with a stainless-steel carafe, four cups, an assortment of sugars, and cream. She poured coffee into each of the four china cups. "Thank you, Emily." The black-haired woman in the grey jacket and calf-length skirt swished when she moved to the door, opening it, then closing it with the whispering click of a metal lock.

Lane leaned forward to add cream and sugar to his coffee. The bone china chimed a pleasant tune when he stirred. He leaned back, sipping, and looked at Joseph. *You called this meeting. What do you want?*

"Thank you for coming. This is a bit of a difficult situation, as I'm sure you all realize." Joseph smiled, leaning forward to add cream to his coffee.

You've got that voice. That motivational speaker voice. You used to read those self-help books and listen to all of the recordings by evangelical gurus who say money and success come from a winning attitude. Lane felt his defences rising.

"What do you want?" Christine looked at the coffee cup in front of her, then at Lane and Arthur.

"Yes, what do you want?" Arthur locked his fingers together, holding them under his chin.

"Good idea. Let's get right to it." Joseph straightened his tie, undid the button on his suit jacket, took a sip of coffee, then set the cup down. "Alison has authorized me to speak with you and to share the details of an initial diagnosis by the psychiatrist."

Lane heard Christine's sharp intake of breath, and he looked at her. She was focused entirely on Joseph.

Joseph noted her reaction and smiled. "Alison, my sister —" he glanced at Lane "— has been diagnosed with bipolar disorder." He looked around the table as if expecting questions. None were forthcoming. "She is beginning to undergo treatment and is on medication."

Too bad there isn't a drug to cure me, Lane thought.

"The psychiatrist is concerned because she is experiencing very severe depression after being excommunicated from Paradise. She has been cut off from her children and extended family. She also faces the prospect of being incarcerated." Joseph looked around the table.

Emotions rose from the soles of Lane's feet. He took a deep breath. Arthur glanced Lane's way. Lane felt the touch of his partner's hand on his shoulder, felt tears welling in his eyes.

"The psychiatrist believes a significant aspect of her

recovery would be regular and supervised contact with you —" he nodded at Christine "— and her grandson."

Christine opened her mouth. Joseph held up his hand.

Lane stood, his body shaking with his voice. "Either Christine speaks now and whenever she sees fit, or we're out of here!"

Christine looked up at Lane. He expected shock. Instead he was greeted by her smile. Lane looked at his brother, who had sunk back into the leather of his wingback chair. His face was almost as white as his shirt.

"Of course." Joseph looked at Christine. "What did you wish to say?"

"Where is Sarah?"

"She chose to return to Paradise. The RCMP arrested Efram Milton at the border. He is facing numerous charges. Sarah returned to Paradise with the other girl. As I said, your mother has been excommunicated." Joseph looked sideways at Lane.

"I know what it's like to be excommunicated." Christine leaned forward, lifting her cup.

"It's very noble of you to be so concerned for your sister," Arthur said to Joseph.

Christine and Lane heard the irony in his voice, turning to watch the exchange.

Joseph shrugged and smiled. "She's family."

Arthur leaned forward. "Yes, family is very important. Especially when one of its members is ruthlessly and cold-bloodedly cut off from the rest of the family."

Joseph set his cup down, looking at Arthur. "Yes. Her doctor said the psychological impact of this kind of isolation often results in serious depression. The doctor believes moving forward like this will help her recovery."

"So you're saying what's done is done, and we should all learn to accept that?" Arthur looked directly at Joseph.

"Yes, absolutely. Alison needs our support." Joseph buttoned his jacket, then unbuttoned it. He looked around nervously as if for the first time sensing he'd fallen into a trap.

Why do I feel sorry for you, Joseph?

"That's it, then?" Christine asked.

"What?" Joseph asked.

"We're not going to discuss what really happened?" Christine asked.

"I'm not sure what you mean?" Joseph looked at Lane as if asking where Christine was going with this.

Lane shrugged, waiting.

Christine said, "My mother was losing her status in Paradise. Does that report also say my mother is going though menopause?"

Joseph blushed.

"I saw this happen before. The woman who escaped Paradise with me experienced the same thing. She was the first wife, but her husband kept getting younger wives. She saw what her daughter's future was going to be like and she left. My mother saw she was being replaced by younger pussy and looked for a way to restore her position in the community. The attempted abduction of my son was the result. I saw the way Milton looked at the girls my age. He had this predatory expression when he saw a young woman he wanted for a wife. I saw the fuck chart in the bishop's office. My name was on it. It took me a while after being away from Paradise to figure out what it all meant. That's why Milton was going south. He was going to trade Sarah for another young wife and sanctuary in another polygamist compound. That's how it works, you know. Maybe you don't want to admit it —" she pointed at Joseph "— but that's what was really going on."

"Be that as it may..." Joseph held the index finger of his right hand in the air as if trying to make a point.

Christine said, "You didn't ask how your brother is doing."

Joseph blushed, looked at Lane, and said nothing.

"You never once asked how my Uncle Paul is feeling. He just saved the lives of four people and you didn't ask how he's feeling or what it cost him." Christine stood up. "We'll go home and discuss this with my family and get back to you. Do you have a business card?"

Arthur and Lane stood.

Joseph got up, walked to his desk, and took a card from a brass holder.

Christine led the way out the door. They were gathering their coats at the front desk when Joseph caught up to them, handing Christine his card. "I know your mother will very much appreciate your cooperation in this matter." He looked sideways at the receptionist.

Christine took the card, stuffing it in her coat pocket. "We'll get back to you." She turned, took Lane by one elbow, Arthur by another, then asked, "Would you please get the door for us, Mr. Lane?"

It took Joseph a full thirty seconds to realize she was talking to him.

When they were in the car, Christine sat in the passenger seat, turned so she could see both of them, and said, "My vote is we take Indy to see my mother."

"What?" Lane turned on the engine.

"Just listen," Arthur said.

"She's not going anywhere for a while. The visits will be supervised, and for once she will have to listen to me. I'll make it clear to her if she doesn't behave herself, Indy and I will leave." Christine turned, facing forward. "Besides, she's still my mother."

A mother who gave up on you. Lane looked over his shoulder as he backed up.

Christine looked sideways at Lane. "I know what you're thinking. She gave up on me, and she gave up on you."

"It's hard going through this again and again with her. It's always a train wreck." Lane stopped, shifting into drive. He checked his mirrors and over his shoulder. *Shit, Christine! Don't you know she will never change?*

"I think you told me once it was never boring being around me." Christine looked down at a wet spot on her blouse. "Can we go home? I'm leaking. It's time to feed Indy."

ACKNOWLEDGEMENTS

Doctors Bruce, Shameem, and Navaid, thank you.

Again, thanks to Tony Bidulka and Wayne Gunn.

Thank you to the staff at Pages Books on Kensington.

Mary, Alex, and Sebi, thanks for the Central Blends suggestions and feedback.

Paul, Natalie, Doug, Jenna, Leslie, Cathy, Matt, and Tiiu: thanks for all that you do. Leslie, this novel is much better because of your sharp eyes and quick mind.

Thank you to Matt at the Shooting Edge.

Thank you, Sara, for the police service background information. And to Dave for police procedural advice.

Thank you Stephen at Sage Innovations for garryryan.ca.

Thanks to creative writers at Nickle, Bowness, Lord Beaverbrook, Alternative, Forest Lawn, and Queen Elizabeth.

As always, thank you to Sharon, Karma, Ben, Luke, Indiana, and Ella.

In 2004, Garry Ryan published his first Detective Lane novel, *Queen's Park*. The second, *The Lucky Elephant Restaurant*, won a 2007 Lambda Literary Award. He has since published six more titles in the series: *A Hummingbird Dance*, *Smoked*, *Malabarista*, *Foxed*, *Glycerine*, and *Indiana Pulcinella*. In 2009, Ryan was awarded Calgary's Freedom of Expression Award. He has also begun a series of World War II adventure novels, with *Blackbirds* and *Two Blackbirds*.